HIS FOR
Christmas

A SPICY CHRISTMAS NOVELLA

LEA ROSE

Copyright © 2024 by Lea Rose

All rights reserved.

No portion of this book may be reproduced in any form without written permission from the publisher or author, except as permitted by U.S. copyright law.

The story, all names, characters, and incidents portrayed in this production are fictitious. No identification with actual persons (living or deceased), places, buildings, and products is intended or should be inferred.

Editing by Steph White (Kat's Literary Services)

Proofreading by Louise Murphy (Kat's Literary Services)

Introduction

Fair warning: this story doesn't waste much time. It's fast, intense, and jumps straight into the deep end of insta-lust and insta-love.

Playlist

Little Mix - Love Me Like You (Christmas Mix)
Ariana Grande - December
BURY & Beneld - FEEL
Chris Brown - No Time Like Christmas
BURY & Omido & Beneld - Good Girl
Montell Fish - Bathroom
Sia - Snowman
Mellina Tey - Before I Move On
Ariana Grande - Wit It This Christmas
Taylor Swift - Snow On The Beach
Britney Spears x Ginuwine x Altégo - Toxic Pony
Sabrina Carpenter - A Nonsense Christmas

To those dreaming of finding a dirty-talking, inked-up powerhouse of a man who fucks you like he owns you underneath the Christmas tree this year—this one's for you.

Chapter 1

Sydney

"I'm telling you right now, if Michael B. Jordan isn't under my Christmas tree in a few weeks, I'm going to lose my shit," my best friend dramatically declares while stirring a pot of marshmallows behind the counter of her cozy little café.

We're working on perfecting the ultimate hot chocolate, and I've made sure to stock up on all the fancy toppings that every child dreams of—whipped cream, candy canes, shaved chocolate, and the kind of sprinkles that make every kid's face light up like it's Christmas morning.

"I'll take any guy who isn't an asshole, doesn't wear a wedding band, and doesn't have some weird need to control me." While we stand with our backs toward the door, I add, "Oh, and a big dick would be nice but not essential so long as he knows how to use it."

"I hear you, girl." We both share a laugh, but it dies instantly when we hear the low, unmistakable sound of a throat clearing behind us.

Cora and I freeze, our eyes meeting in that split second of mutual *oh-shit* realization. Neither of us says a word, but it's all there in the wide-eyed, slightly panicked stare we exchange.

My mind races, silently praying to the universe that the customer standing behind us didn't hear the words that just tumbled out of my mouth. But as I turn, the sight before me is absolutely devastating. I'm met with a face so chiseled and flawless that it looks like it's been sculpted by a god, and when his lips curve into a slow, knowing smile, it's painfully clear that he heard every damn word.

He has the kind of face that makes you want to slide your hand into your panties at three in the morning.

Can you tell it's been months since I last had sex? With thoughts like that, I may as well hold a neon sign above my head that reads "NEEDS A GOOD FUCKING."

The guy with the full, sinful lips towers over me, easily surpassing six feet, making me feel small in comparison, and I never feel small when I'm a long-legged five foot eight and a half.

His fitted white button-up shirt clings to every curve and contour of his chest, outlining the hard muscle beneath like it was tailored for temptation. His broad arms stretch the sleeves just enough to hint at their strength, drawing my eyes to the way each button strains slightly with every breath he takes.

My mind drifts—*oh, how it drifts*—to the thought of him effortlessly lifting me with those arms, maybe pinning me against a wall, or tossing me onto a bed like I weigh nothing. You know, the completely casual thoughts that come to mind when faced with a man who looks like every book boyfriend I've ever had.

But it's his piercing gray eyes that capture me. They draw me in, locking onto mine with an intensity that's impossible to ignore. A light layer of stubble accentuates his chiseled jawline, only adding to his rugged yet entirely put-together appearance.

His whole look screams, "I could ruin your life, and you'd thank me for it."

Cora—ever the professional—welcomes him with her perfect, practiced smile as if he hadn't just heard our entire conversation and says, "Good morning, sir. What can I get for you today?"

"I'm actually meeting someone, so I was hoping I could grab a table before I order," he says, flashing Cora a polite smile that doesn't quite reach his steel eyes.

However, when his gaze shifts back to me, there's something more there—something that catches me and holds me in place.

"I promise I'm not just trying to escape the cold."

Oh god, he has dimples.

It's December in New York, and the crowded streets are packed with people bundled up in layers. Although snow hasn't fallen yet, it's fucking freezing out there, and I can't blame anyone for wanting to get inside somewhere warm. Anything beats being out there, braving the streets of the city that never stops shivering in winter.

"Of course. Just come back up when you're ready," Cora replies as I stand beside her, staring at him like a dumbass.

Pull yourself together. You're not the girl who lusts after a guy just because he has a pretty face—a face that would make one hell of a throne.

Cora steps out from behind the counter and heads toward a table where two elegant, silver-haired women have just settled in. Meanwhile, tall, dark, and dangerously handsome keeps his gaze locked on me.

Marvel gave us Captain America.

The universe gave us him.

"The things you're looking for in a guy aren't unrealistic. If you keep your standards high, then maybe you'll stop rolling around with assholes." For the second time in the last five minutes, I'm at a loss for words.

Do you know what every single guy who walks this planet has in common? Dumb fucking misplaced bravery.

He pushes himself off the counter, the corners of his lips curling into a smug smile, and no matter how pretty it is, I have the sudden urge to slap it off his face.

"I'm Edison Miller, by the way," he says, extending his hand to me.

My eyes drop to where his hand hangs in the space between us, and I'm immediately drawn to the large black rose tattoo inked on his skin. When I return my gaze to his, he cocks his head slightly, grinning down at me from that six-foot-everything height, like he's fully aware he's just checked off some box on my perfect man wish list. I take his hand and shake it, and when I feel a warm flutter in my stomach, I'm ready to eye-roll myself off a cliff.

However, that warm feeling low in my belly isn't the kind that wraps you up and makes you feel safe. It's an all-consuming heat that licks across your skin like flames from hell.

"I'm Sydney. It's nice to meet you," I finally reply with a smile as his large hand engulfs mine, lingering for a moment longer than a normal handshake should. "And that's Cora," I add, nodding toward her across the café, her caramel curls catching the light and practically glowing like liquid gold against her rich, dark skin.

"So this is your place?" he asks, his eyes tracking Cora as she makes her way back around the counter. "It's nice in here."

"Thank you," she says, her hazel eyes glinting with flecks of gold as she flashes a proud smile.

"Anyway, I appreciate the warm welcome, ladies. I'll order once my date arrives."

In the space of a few minutes, this guy has flipped me upside down, leaving me shamelessly staring at his ass as he walks away like I'm some kind of low-key pervert.

He heads straight for the most secluded table in the corner, right beside a small Christmas tree adorned with white twinkling lights—my only contribution to the festive decor Cora has put up in here this year.

Cora edges closer to me, her shoulder brushing against mine as she leans in and speaks quietly into my ear, "I changed my mind, Syd. I think I want him to be under my tree."

"I think you might have some competition." I nod toward the door as a stunning brunette walks in.

Her sleek ponytail bounces behind her as she confidently makes her way over to Edison's table. I can only imagine the cost of her clothes, considering she practically screams designer labels. From the dark-gray coat to the diamond studs in her ears that sparkle like little reminders that she's in a whole other tax bracket. I can practically feel the weight of the price tag on her outfit, and I'd bet it's worth more than everything I own combined.

I watch as Edison rises from his seat to greet his date, leaning in to press a kiss to each cheek, but on the second one, his eyes find mine from across the room. For a brief moment, I hold his gaze, my stomach doing the smallest flip before I turn back to Cora.

"Lucky bitch," I whisper half jokingly, though the faint twist of envy I feel isn't entirely fake.

"Right!" Cora laughs as she playfully nudges me.

Cora's Café sits in the heart of New York City. I spend most of my days here, and I wouldn't have it any other way. I love that I get to work with one of my favorite people in the world—Cora, my best friend, ride or die, part-time therapist, occasional pain in my ass, and probably my soulmate. We've been inseparable since middle school, made it through all the high school drama, and now I work with her here.

Part-time anyway.

I glance up from the counter and notice Edison striding confidently toward us. His shoulders are squared, and his muscles tighten beneath his shirt.

"I'm going to slip out back and grab some milk. You good with him?" Cora asks, raising an eyebrow at me, with a knowing smile playing on her lips. "He's into you, by the way," she adds casually, like it's the most obvious thing in the world before she saunters off.

"He's on a date," I grit out almost silently through clenched teeth, knowing she can't hear me and that this guy has annoyingly good hearing.

I turn back to face him, my gaze dropping to where his hands rest on the counter, fingers splayed out.

"Do you know what you want?" I ask as the air charges between us.

His eyes hold mine as a lazy smile tugs at the corner of his lips like he's weighing up his options. "I've seen a couple of things I want, but first, I'd like to order a hot chocolate and a cappuccino, please."

"Would you like me to bring them over?"

"No, thank you. I'm happy to wait."

"You sure?" I smile at him, my lips curling upward as I raise an eyebrow in question. He nods, and I turn to the coffee machine, quickly steaming and frothing milk for their drinks. I can feel his eyes burning into me, and I bite the inside of my cheek to stop myself from glancing back at him.

"So, how long have you lived in New York?" he asks, his voice cutting through the hissing of the coffee machine.

"My accent doesn't give it away?"

"Have you ever heard of small talk?" he taunts, eyes finding mine again as I spin around to face him.

"I've heard of it, but I can't say I'm a fan. However, for you, I'll play." He lets out a low chuckle, and I feel an unfamiliar tightness coil in my stomach. As I turn away from him again, I ask, "So what do you do?"

"My job isn't all that exciting. I built a company from scratch, and now I spend most of my time signing paperwork."

"Okay, so you have money and power. Got it," I blurt out, the words escaping me before I can slap a filter on them. When he doesn't respond right away, I force myself to turn back around and find that he's watching me.

"I'm a normal guy, Sydney."

"If you say so." I shrug, trying to hide my disdain for wealthy men.

"If you're so sure about the type of guy I am, why don't you let me take you out and prove you wrong?"

Is. He. Serious?

My jaw drops, and my hand lands on my hip as I stare at him in disbelief. "You did not just ask me out while you're on a date with another woman." My eyes widen, half expecting him to backtrack, but the expression on his face tells me he has absolutely no intention of doing so.

See, dumb fucking misplaced bravery.

"I knew within a minute of meeting her that this would be our only date."

"Wow. Seriously, wow." This time my words come with an incredulous laugh because... what the actual fuck?

"What?" he asks.

"First off, are you blind? Your date is probably the most beautiful woman I've ever seen."

"Agree to disagree. Besides, I'm looking for more than that. So can I take you for dinner tonight?"

"Hard pass, but thank you for the offer. Besides, I'm working tonight."

"You're working now."

"I have two jobs. Not all of us have the luxury of just signing our names for a living." I catch the hint of a smirk on his lips, but he masks it quickly.

"Okay, so when do you get off tonight?" he pushes.

"Late. I'm talking like two a.m. late."

I set his drinks in front of him, and he slides his card across to me as if we're in the middle of some business transaction—which we technically are—and not this back and forth.

"Are you a nurse?"

I tilt my head from side to side as though I'm considering his question. "Only when asked."

He chuckles, and a smile pulls at his lips. "Okay, you gotta give me something here," he says, leaning in a little like he's trying to close the distance that I'm putting between us.

"No, I don't," I reply. "Now, take your drinks to your date before she dies of thirst." He smiles, and there they are—two dimples reappearing, adding a touch of softness to his sharp features. He lifts the two mugs, but he lingers, trying to prolong the moment between us as we continue this playful game of push and pull across the counter.

"I know you don't know me, Sydney, but I always get what I want," he warns before walking away without another word.

Money equals power.

Asshole.

He might have tattoos and no wedding band, but I'm not going down the same path I went down with my ex-boyfriend Charlie. If the flag looks red, then it probably is, and ignoring those warnings will only bite you in the ass later.

Edison and his date remain for another half an hour. When they finally stand up to leave, I keep my eyes focused on anything but him, pretending to be absorbed in wiping the already gleaming counter. But then I feel it—that pull—it's like an awareness, and when I glance up, his eyes find mine one last time as he heads for the door.

And damn it, I hate that I don't hate the way he looks at me.

Chapter 2

Sydney

The Dancing Lilacs isn't your average gentleman's club—it's high-end and exclusive, and I'm well aware of how fortunate I am compared to others in the same line of work who don't receive this level of care—or this paycheck.

I've been working here for a few years now. Is it my dream job? No, not even close. I didn't wake up one day thinking, *"Do you know what sounds like the American dream? pole dancing."*

The whole idea of a "dream job" has always felt a little overrated to me anyway. As a kid, I really wanted to be Britney Spears—but who didn't? Apart from that, I didn't have a lifelong calling or a grand career plan, and I think that's okay to admit.

This job pays my bills, keeps a roof over my head, and allows me to splurge on the things I want without feeling guilty about it. Plus, it gives me the freedom to do what I want with my free time without being chained to some nine-to-five grind.

Okay, so it isn't always glamorous. I have to deal with my fair share of assholes, but sometimes life is messy no matter who you are, and honestly, most of us are just out here winging it and doing the best we can.

All we can do is take a deep breath, remind ourselves who the fuck we are, and then go handle things like the badass we were born to be.

The men who come here don't just wear their wealth—they flaunt it, dripping in designer suits, with more money than they could ever spend. These men, with their perfect lives and picture-perfect wives—wives who probably have no idea what goes on behind closed doors and who most likely don't know how far their husbands are willing to go in a place like this—are something to watch. Inside these walls, their darkest cravings come alive, masked by expensive cologne and the weight of their power.

Here, vows are shattered, and commitment no longer exists.

Surrounded by rich gold and black décor, I take in the dressing room—the floor-to-ceiling mirrors reflect every angle, capturing who I am and the person I'm about to become. I breathe in, letting the atmosphere settle over me as I prepare to slip into the role men pay to see, stepping into a version of myself that feels both familiar and distant, dark and controlled, a side of me that only comes alive within these walls, designed to make them ache.

And the best part is watching their desperation play out, knowing they'll never get close enough to really touch.

Looking through my options, I finally slip into a black lace lingerie set that clings to every curve. I add a sheer skirt that barely skims my hips, so transparent that it leaves almost nothing to the imagination, before finishing my outfit with a pair of sky-high heels that emphasize my already long legs. My blonde hair cascades down my back in loose waves, falling just above my waist, and with one final touch, I spritz on my favorite perfume.

As soon as I enter the club's main area, I'm immersed in a deep-green and gold haze. The décor is pure luxury, with a seductive burlesque avant-garde vibe that oozes sophistication—which is ironic considering what goes on here behind the illusion of elegance.

Gold tables and chairs are scattered around the room while large green velvet curtains drape from the ceiling, creating a sense of intimacy as they separate different areas of the club. Peeking behind them are poles and raised podiums, where I'll inevitably find myself dancing at some point tonight.

I've been here long enough that my role has shifted from dancer to hostess. I used to be up on the stage four or five times a night, dancing under the lights until my legs ached. But now I'm down to just one performance, and then that part of the night is behind me.

Now, I mostly get to work the floor, weaving through the room, and entertaining men with conversation while wearing an outfit that holds their attention and keeps them coming back for more.

But those conversations have played a big part in why I've started to pull back from men.

Sex I enjoy, but relationships are not for me.

Seeing the worst of the male species in a place like this—how easily their eyes wander, how quick they are to forget their wedding bands, and how willing they are to spend a small fortune for a fleeting moment of attention—has changed something in me.

It isn't lost on me that I'm part of the problem, but I'd never cross a line with any of the men here. I have my boundaries, and I keep them firmly in place. My job is to keep their interest piqued, to play the part I learned to master but never get caught up in it.

And after what I went through with my ex-boyfriend, I decided that love is bullshit, and working somewhere like here only reinforces that belief. Especially when these men don't even bother to remove their wedding bands when they're paying for a blowjob from one of the other girls in a private room—yeah, it happens more than you'd think.

What they do for a little extra cash is up to them, but I have never, and will never, allow any of these men to touch me.

"Hey, Sydney," Tanya calls out to me.

With her long, sleek black hair draping like silk against her olive skin, the woman behind the bar is effortlessly stunning and has the most perfect pair of fake breasts I think I've ever seen or touched, for that matter.

Because we're friends and I was curious.

"Can I please get some water? I've got the pole in a little while," I say, leaning against the bar.

Tanya nods and spins around, pouring water into a glass with a few ice cubes to at least create the illusion that I'm standing here drinking something alcoholic.

As I take a sip and scan the crowded club, my heart stops when my gaze lands on the entrance. A tall figure stands silhouetted against the golden glow of the lights, but even through the haze, I can see exactly who it is.

What. In. The. Fuck?

Edison Miller—who is, without a doubt, most women's walking wet dream—confidently walks through the club, commanding attention in an all-black suit that clings to his body like it was tailor-made for him—hell, it probably was.

My mouth goes dry at the sight of him, and my pulse quickens with every step he takes. Heads turn, and whispers follow as he moves through the crowd because he's just that devastatingly handsome.

His eyes sweep every corner of the club as if he's searching for something—or someone—until they finally land on me. The moment his dark and determined gaze locks onto mine, a slow smirk plays across his lips, one that says he's found exactly what he was looking for. There's no surprise on his face, only the satisfaction that I'm precisely where he expected me to be.

He's playing a game that I didn't even know I was a part of, and he's already ten steps ahead.

Edison is rooted in place, daring me with his eyes to approach him, so I march my almost-naked ass over to find out how the hell he tracked me down. Each step I take is deliberate, and I feel the weight of his stare. But I know the power I hold in this room, and I won't allow him to strip me of it.

"It's nice to see you again, Sydney," he says with a smile.

"It's nice to see you, too, Edison. What brings you here?" I reply, my voice dripping with sarcasm as I flash him a fake-ass smile. His smirk widens, clearly enjoying the challenge, but I hold my ground. If he thought he was going to walk in here and throw me off my game, he's sorely mistaken. Here, I'm in control, and he's just another man trying to get a taste of what he can't have.

"I was driving nearby and thought I'd drop in."

"That right?"

He inches closer to me, barely grazing my body with his own. The tension simmers, and a raw heat between us builds as my body hovers dangerously close to almost crossing the club's strict no-touching rule.

"I told you, Sydney, I always get what I want," he whispers in my ear, his promise laced with desire.

"And what is it you want, considering I've turned you down once today already?"

"You made a mistake."

"I have no intention of dating you, so you're wasting your time."

"Agree to disagree," he says as he walks straight past me.

My mouth hanging open, I turn to catch a glimpse of him weaving through the crowd toward the bar at the center of the room. Just as I lose sight of him, a voice snaps me back to reality.

"Hey, Sydney, you're up next in bay two," Coco, one of the other dancers, calls out, relaying Ash's message.

Our boss, Asher Crane, is always here at the club, overseeing everything. Even though he could easily employ someone else to run the place while he drinks cocktails on a private beach, Ash chooses to stay.

I give Coco a quick nod while I get my shit together and head toward the pole. I pass by Edison on my way to one of the curtained-off areas, and as I step inside, a group of men sit in a circle of plush emerald chairs around a gold pole in the center of the room.

Most of the faces sitting here staring back are familiar to me now, but tonight, there's one new face that I didn't expect to see when I turned up for my shift. His face has been haunting me since the moment I first laid eyes on him today.

I'm torn between being impressed that he went to such lengths to find me and feeling a little uneasy because his actions are giving off some serious stalker vibes.

I wonder if he has a mask...

I snap out of my masked man fantasy as soon as "Bathroom" by Montell Fish starts to play.

Closing my eyes, I surrender myself to the music and feel its energy seep into my skin. I take a slow, deep breath as I gracefully hook my stiletto heel around the cool metal pole, and my body undulates as I lose myself in the moment. As I arch my back, my head tilts backward in a smooth arc, and my long platinum hair brushes the curve of my ass. My fingers glide through the strands, and I can't help but imagine what it would feel like to have it wrapped around Edison's inked fist.

I sway and twist around the pole, my body gliding effortlessly, showing off everything my mama gave me.

The crowd of men watches me, but my focus narrows to one person—Edison. His eyes, like stormy rain clouds, are dark and filled with a deep, consuming lust that sets fire to every part of me. It's as if he's dragging me into the depths of hell itself, his stare an irresistible vortex of darkness that I can't escape.

His body is completely at ease, his long legs stretched out in front of his chair. But when I spin and dip, I notice his hands. The way his fingers grip the chair's arms reveals how affected he is by me at this moment.

I slink around the pole with slow and sensual movements, and as I reach the floor, I lower myself to all fours. I start to crawl toward the circle of men sitting in their chairs, their eyes glued to my every move. The smug smile on my face is purely for them. It's a performance, a show of submission that's anything but. They may think they have control because I'm on my hands and knees, but little do they know that I have all the power. This act is my choice, my control; I'm the puppeteer here, and they, unknowingly, are the puppets.

I crawl toward Edison, every inch of me focused on him until I'm right in front of his chair. He leans forward, his elbows resting on his knees, while I slowly kneel on mine. I part my legs just enough to guarantee I have his full attention while my hands roam over my body, tracing every edge before I rise to my feet.

With a sway of my hips, I move back toward the pole, and I can feel the heat of his gaze trailing after me. Every movement is a deliberate seduction meant to captivate and command the room, and when I turn and catch those deep-silver eyes watching me, I find myself unable to look away.

Chapter 3

Sydney

As the music fades and the song ends, I make a graceful exit and return to the dressing room. Thankfully, my turn on the pole is over for tonight. But honestly, I'm not in the mood to walk around the club massaging the egos of rich assholes.

I don't want to hear a word about Jeffrey Warner's new yacht or how "fabulous" I would look perched on the edge of it with a glass of overpriced champagne. I have zero interest in hearing how much money Oliver Black has raked in from his latest venture into luxury men's bath soap—apparently, even shower gel needs a designer label. I don't give a flying shit about any of it, and yet my night will be spent nodding along to every tedious, self-indulgent detail, pretending to be impressed, while fighting the urge to roll my eyes into another dimension.

Edison must be loaded.

You'd have to be to get into a place like this, where even breathing feels like a luxury you're being billed for.

How the hell did he pass the checks so fast?

How did he track me down when he only knew my first name?
Raging psycho.
An unfairly hot psycho, the kind that looks like bad decisions wrapped in muscle and ink, drawing me in like a moth to a beautifully tattooed flame.

Ideally, Edison will have left by the time I reach the club's main area, and I won't have to spend the night watching and waiting for him to pounce.

I also won't spend the rest of the night looking around for the crazy person I'm stupidly attracted to.

With my practiced, almost painfully fake grin back on my face, I glide around the room, smiling at these men and leading them to believe they're exactly the kind of men who could get me off. I tilt my head, laugh at all the right moments, and lean in just close enough to let them feel a spark that I'm never going to feel, one that only exists in their heads.

I feel the weight of their stares, catch the flicker in their eyes—the look that says they think they've got me hooked, like they're one suave comment away from breaking through.

In reality, they repulse me.

It's not so much about their appearance—though clearly, I have a weakness for tall, tatted, and trouble.

I make my way to the bar, and Tanya turns to me with a grin, holding out a glass filled with ice and water. "Here, water on the rocks," she quips, and I laugh as I take the drink. But as I'm about to take a sip, I suddenly feel a solid wall press against my back.

Edison.

His scent engulfs me, intoxicating and unmistakably masculine—like spice and sin wrapped in heat. I have no idea what it is, but it's pure man, and I silently curse my treacherous vagina as heat coils low in my belly, betraying me with a need I didn't ask for.

The sound of my own heart pounding in my ears almost drowns out the club noise as he leans in closer, his breath hot against my neck, causing an involuntary shiver. "Can I get you something a little stronger?"

"No, thank you," I reply, quickly turning to face him. "I'm working."

"You keep saying that to me."

This fucking guy.

"How did you find me?"

Edison smirks—his infuriatingly cocky expression spreads across his face as he runs a hand over his stubbled jawline, clearly satisfied with himself.

"As I mentioned earlier, if I want something, I find a way to get it. You didn't want to tell me where you were working tonight, so I had to figure it out."

"You realize how creepy that is, don't you?"

"I value my time and I don't waste it. It took me an hour to find out that you, Sydney Thorne, work here. So maybe to you, it's creepy, but to me, it's being efficient and getting what I want faster than playing a game with you, where I have to wait for you to inevitably tell me."

"Are you a cop?" I ask, and he laughs—a low, throaty sound that irritates me as much as it makes me want to swallow it with my mouth. However, I'm not in the mood for games, and I just need to know what the hell is happening here.

"No, I'm not a cop. I'm the owner of Miller Security, and I happen to know a lot of people, so you denying me was a waste of time."

"That's how you got in here so easily."

"Ash and I go way back. I oversee security for this club, which you're obviously aware of, as well as many others in the city."

"I'm guessing you were given free access to get in here tonight?"

"It wasn't free, but it was easy, yes."

He's gotta be crazy.

His face draws closer, and his lips brush against my ear, sending shivers down my spine as his breath caresses my skin. "I would've gladly paid twice as much to watch you dance for me like that tonight," he murmurs, his voice dripping with sex while I'm just dripping.

"There were a lot of men in that room. That show wasn't just for you."

"Yes, it fucking was, and we both know it."

"I don't even know you."

"So, let's change that."

Get me away from this temptation.

"You'll have to excuse me. I have to work, and despite what you believe, you're not the only guy here tonight." He smiles, the corners of his lips twisting up in amusement. "Other men pay to have my attention, so if you're bored, I'll happily find one of the other girls for you, and they'll entertain you."

I attempt to step past him to put some physical distance between us, but suddenly his hand wraps around my waist, strong and possessive, those controlled fingers pressing firmly against my skin, holding me exactly where he wants me. "Don't even think about finding someone else for me," he growls, his tone thick with warning. "And in case you weren't aware, there's no one here for you tonight except me."

My mind races to connect the dots, and when it finally clicks, the realization of what he's done hits me like a punch to the gut.

My eyes widen, and I shake my head in disbelief. "You didn't..." I trail off, the words catching in my throat, unable to finish my sentence as anger floods my veins.

"I gave Ash a donation so you could take the rest of the night off."

"You mean you bought me?" I spit out as my hands ball up into fists by my sides. He stares down at me, his expression giving away absolutely nothing. "Do I look like I have a fucking price tag on me, Edison? Jesus." His gaze fixes on me as if he's trying to figure out how to handle me and how to calm the fire he's ignited. "What did you pay?"

"Not nearly enough."

And, of course, the bastard is unapologetic as fuck.

"Awesome. So what am I to you tonight, huh? Your damn pet?"

"If that's what you think is happening here, then you're moving even faster than I am," he answers with a smirk that I'm ready to slap the shit out of.

"This isn't funny."

"Never said it was, beautiful."

"You don't get rejected often, do you? Because this isn't how you pursue a woman."

"You don't think so?" he teases, and I can feel my frustration growing.

"No, but I assume that it worked out for you before, based on your arrogance."

"I tried the old-fashioned approach this morning, didn't I?"

"You did, and I said no."

"I didn't like that answer." His chin dips once more, and his voice lowers to a near whisper. "Besides, what do you expect me to think when your body is practically screaming yes?" His fingers trace along the curve of my hip, and I hate how my body betrays me as I tremble under his touch. "Your stomach has clenched seven times. Your nipples are straining against this extremely thin fabric, and your cheeks are flushed." He pauses, taking a deep breath, yet I feel like he's just stolen all of mine. "Now tell me you're not even remotely interested in finding out why, despite being clearly pissed, you're still attracted to me."

"I'm not attracted to arrogant assholes who believe they can buy me," I bite out, pushing myself away from him and breaking free of this pull.

"Yet you're surrounded by them here."

"And I have never dated a single one of them."

"Until now."

"This is not a date," I snap at him.

"Then call it whatever you want, but you're not a purchase. Do you understand me? You're free to leave whenever you want."

"Good to know," I reply with a nod, refusing to give him anything more before turning on my heel and heading straight for the dressing room. I waste no time throwing on the clothes I arrived in before grabbing my coat and making my way to the club's back door.

Slipping out unnoticed, I step into the cold night air, the chill instantly biting at my skin. I don't stop walking, driven by the urge to create as much distance as possible from Edison, from the club—all of it.

However, as I turn the corner and approach the club's entrance, what unfolds in front of me doesn't even shock me. Edison Miller casually leans against a sleek black car, its engine idling quietly, his ankles crossed in front of him, and a no-fucks-given expression settles on his face.

"Really?" I ask, my one word laced with sarcasm.

"I'm trying not to take it personally that you bailed on me, but I'm definitely not letting you go home alone. Come on—my driver will take you."

My mom would tell me to keep walking, to never step into a car with a guy I barely know, but my stupid side—the side that's drawn to tattoos and dimples—will always win.

I can see the headlines now.

"Family grieves as their only daughter's tragic death leaves them heartbroken right before Christmas. According to reports, she willingly entered a vehicle with an attractive man, despite him being a walking red fucking flag."

"Fine."

I'm an idiot.

With hesitant steps, I approach him as he waits by the car door. As I get close, he extends his hand as if it's the most natural thing in the world for me to take it.

Which, of course, I do.

His hand is warm, his grip firm, and as his fingers close around mine, I find myself briefly lost in how intimate this simple touch feels.

As I slide into the car, the rich scent of expensive leather mixed with just a hint of bourbon lingers in the air. The heated seats work their magic, melting away the chill that clings to me as I sink into their softness. The interior practically sparkles, every surface is perfectly polished, and a bottle of top-shelf bourbon sits in the center console. Tinted windows wrap us in complete privacy, and the raised divider between us and the driver ensures that this moment is ours.

Edison joins me in the back and closes the door with a gentle thud. "I assume you and the driver already know where I live," I state, not asking but merely acknowledging what I already know to be true.

"I'm very efficient."

"No, you're crazy."

"If I were crazy, do you really think you should be calling me that? It could push me over the edge." That silences me completely, but he immediately begins to laugh. "Come on, humor me until we get back to your place, and I swear I won't bother you again if you don't want to rip my clothes off by the time we get there."

"You promise?"

"I promise, Sydney. Just give me a chance to get to know you. That's all I'm asking."

"Fine. You get three questions."

"And you'll answer them all honestly?" I nod, bracing myself for whatever's coming next. "Do you enjoy dancing for men, or are you there for the money?" The question leaves his lips without a hint of hesitation. I knew he wouldn't go easy on me, but I wasn't expecting him to be so direct.

"A part of me enjoys being watched. I like the way it makes me feel, the power in holding a room's attention, but I don't particularly like the men who come to the club, so I'm mostly there because it pays well, and it gives me a level of independence I wouldn't have otherwise."

"You're into being watched," he muses, eyebrows raised in curiosity. "Is that true for anything else?"

I tilt my head slightly, a smile tugging at the corners of my lips. "Is that your question?"

"No, because I already know the answer."

"Yeah?"

He nods, his gaze never leaving mine. "I'm really good at paying attention to detail. Being able to read people and their body language is essential when it comes to training my team."

"Here I thought you just signed your name a lot."

"That is essentially what my job consists of these days, now that I have people I trust running my shit."

"Next question," I say.

"Would you date me if I were broke?" he asks, triggering a flashback to this morning at Cora's, where I made a snap judgment about him. "Because your energy switched as soon as you assumed I had money."

"I don't think it was an assumption."

"It wasn't, but you made a judgment based on it," he says, his tone firm, and it feels like he's just whacked me with the asshole stick. "Now I'll ask you again. Would you have said yes to dinner with me if I didn't have money?"

"No, because you still asked me out while you were on a date with another woman."

"It was a first date, and I knew right away that there was no spark, no chemistry. We ended the date on good terms after she said she felt the same way." His eyes hungrily trail over my lips, his own full and slightly parted. "It's the opposite of how I felt when I met you," he admits. "And I tracked you down because I don't remember the last time I felt that spark, and I knew that I needed to know more about you."

"And now you know more. Now you know what I do. Has that changed?"

"The only difference was that I went from calm to wanting to rip out at least fifteen men's spines just so I could watch you dance alone."

"So you're the jealous type?"

"I call it territorial."

"You're an only child, aren't you? I bet you never had to share your toys." The moment the words leave my mouth, a knowing smile spreads across his lips—a silent confirmation, and before I know it, I'm laughing.

"Is it that obvious?"

"Let's just say you don't hide it well."

As the car comes to a stop, I glance out the window at my apartment building, and part of me wishes the driver would just keep circling for a little while longer. I'm not ready to break free from whatever is happening here because as soon as I step out of the car, I know I'll return to the reality of who I am and the walls I maintain.

I move to leave, my hand reaching for the door handle, but before I can pull away, he's suddenly right there, crowding me. He leans in, his breath hot against my ear, sending an involuntarily shudder through me.

"I have one last question," he whispers, his voice low and rough, the kind that curls around your spine.

I turn my face toward his, and his eyes meet mine, blazing with a need that crawls beneath my skin. He pauses for a heartbeat before his focus drops to my lips, the spark between us impossible to ignore.

"Would I find you wet if I slid my hand between your thighs?"

Fuck it.

"You'd find me soaked, Edison Miller," I answer honestly, because being trapped in such close proximity with this guy is fucking lethal, and my days of being young and wild are threatening to resurface.

My pulse kicks up, and I can see the effect my words have on him by the way his teeth graze his bottom lip. The savage look in his eyes makes me want to invite him up to my apartment—and for a split second, I consider it—where we could lose ourselves in each other for the rest of the night. But I know guys like him—they chase until they catch you, then leave you behind like they've completely forgotten you.

"Thanks for the ride," I continue, trying to ignore the fluttering in my stomach. "And for not being as crazy as I thought you might've been."

As I reach for the door again, he yanks me back with a vice-like grip on my arm. Before I can react, his other hand clamps down on the base of my throat, not squeezing but firm enough to hold me in place as he pushes me forcefully back into the seat. His wild eyes fixate on my lips once again, hungry and possessive.

"I don't kiss on a first date," I manage to mumble, but I know it's futile. He's determined to take what we both crave, and I'm powerless to resist.

"This isn't a fucking date."

His lips crash against mine, controlling and dominating every second of our kiss. The swipe of his tongue and his firm grip on my neck, possessive yet passionate all at once, have me desperate for him to get closer. He tastes like a mix of mint, whiskey, and something else—something that's uniquely him, and I want more of it. Deep in his chest, a low growl rumbles, and as he pulls away, we both gasp for air.

I've never been kissed like that before, as if his need to claim me completely overpowered any restraint he might have had. There's no tenderness, only a hunger that's left my heart pounding.

"Get out," he murmurs against my lips, releasing his grip on my throat.

"What?"

"Unless you want my driver to witness me fucking the life out of you right here in my car, I suggest you leave." As he leans back into his seat, my voice falls silent. "I'm not playing, Sydney. I'm two seconds away from letting Gregg hear you scream my name because there's no other way this is going, and we both know it." I bite my lip and can't help but smirk because, while I'm not entirely against the idea, it's obvious he's on edge and frustrated as hell.

"Thanks again for the ride," I say to him before I climb out of the car, feeling the cold air hit my flushed skin. I take a deep breath, steadying myself, before making my way to my apartment.

As soon as I close the door behind me, a burst of uncontrollable giggles escapes my lips because I just kissed trouble—and trouble has never tasted so good.

Chapter 4

Edison

I sit in my living room, still slightly damp from my shower, while a fire crackles, casting a soft glow around the room. The lights are dim, and I'm dressed in nothing but a pair of black boxer briefs.

My phone sits in my hand, and my thumb hovers over Sydney's name on the screen, debating when would be the best time to send her a message.

Or maybe I'll just show up at the club again.

The moment I left the coffee shop, I made it my business to learn everything I could about her—her full name, where she worked, and her address. And yeah, I took her cell number too. It isn't difficult to find information, not when you know where to look, who to ask, and have the right resources. I did a little digging, but with only one goal in mind—to get her to go on a fucking date with me.

I'm not the type of guy to wait around for what he wants.

Patience is overrated.

I saw something in Sydney that drew me in, and I needed more than a few moments with her. Especially when those moments had her reacting to me with an edge I wasn't used to, and yet her hostility only made me want her more.

I needed a way to get her attention.

You'd think I was asking her for a goddamn kidney with how she reacted.

Ever since she called me out for asking her on a date while I was still technically on a date with someone else, I haven't been able to stop thinking about her. Or, more specifically, obsessing over the way her mouth might taste. As I stood across from her, the low hum of coffee machines buzzed in the background, and all I could think about was what it would feel like to press my lips against hers—to silence that mouth that was so quick to put me in my place.

That kiss in my car—it wasn't planned. I did it because I couldn't stop myself; she was too damn tempting, and she made me feel weak in a way that I hadn't before.

However, it wasn't just about my lack of self-control around her.

I kissed her because I needed to show her that I could make her feel something she wouldn't forget any time soon. I wanted her to be left replaying the way my lips moved against hers and how I drew her in, leaving a fire between us that couldn't be ignored. If she felt even a fraction of what I did, she'd find herself craving more, wondering what else I could make her feel.

I felt her attraction to me long before my lips ever touched hers. The way her gaze lingered on my face as I edged closer, her eyes flickering with the question of whether to give in or fight it, made me fucking primal.

With my hand wrapped around her throat, her pulse thrummed beneath my fingers, matching the fierce beat of my own heart. It was the unspoken confirmation I didn't know I was waiting for—her breath hitched, her green eyes darkened, and I knew she felt it too. She was right there with me, caught in the same heady, inescapable pull, waiting for that line between us to fade until nothing else remained.

And god, that girl can kiss.

Even before I saw her face, it was her voice and her list of demands that hooked me. Her long blonde hair fell down her back in soft waves, almost reaching her waist, and my gaze was drawn to the way her blue denim jeans hugged her curvaceous ass. I overheard her talking about the kind of man she did and didn't want, and I sure as hell knew I fit her criteria. When she finally turned around, I saw just how beautiful she was. That immediate attraction rarely happens to me, if ever. But with her, it hit hard, and her initial disinterest only fueled my desire to get to know her better.

What can I say? I'm fucking complicated, and I get off on a challenge.

Since the night I almost had her spread open for me in the back of my car, I've braved the cold and walked past Cora's Café twice now. Both times, Sydney has been busy pouring drinks for customers, completely oblivious to me lurking outside like some kind of crazy-ass stalker.

I watched her smile sweetly at the customers, my satisfaction growing stronger knowing they had no idea of the darkness beneath her innocent facade. There's a side of her that craves power and control, something I took great pleasure in stripping her of when my hand was clasped around her pretty little throat. But the truth is, she liked it. She liked being on the other side of that control, and she enjoyed the way I took it from her.

She might play the part of good girl in the daylight, but there's so much more to her than that.

I saw it.

I felt it.

She has the aura of an angel, yet there's a hint of fire in her soul, and I'm drawn to both sides equally.

Ash, the owner of The Dancing Lilacs, has known me for years. Not only has my company installed all the security cameras in the club, but I also provide him with a security team to work the doors. So when I found out that Sydney was employed there, all it took was a small fee.

Ash couldn't give a flying shit about why I was there, so long as his club continues to run smoothly. Besides, I made sure I was discreet, and I got exactly what I wanted—a front seat to Sydney's world and a side to her that I didn't see when she served me my ass at the café.

Thanks to Ash's text, I found out that Sydney was back at the club tonight. And now that I'm officially a member, I have free rein to come and go as I please.

I need to watch her dance again.

I just need to see her again.

I know I intrigue her, and it's a beautiful feeling when the thirst is mutual.

Since giving up on meaningless sex and women who should come with a fucking warning label, I've been looking for someone with whom, even if my dick fell off, we'd have such raw sexual chemistry that I'd still want her just as fiercely.

I know exactly what I'm looking for—someone who challenges me, someone who matches my fire—and until I know she isn't it, I'm not leaving her alone.

Call me whatever you want, but if she's the one, I'm keeping her. I'm not getting any younger, and at thirty-nine, I'm ready to spend the rest of my life inside one woman.

For a few minutes, I stand outside The Dancing Lilacs, staring up at the building that's lit up like a goddamn Christmas tree—strings of fairy lights twinkle in every window and actual Christmas trees adorn the entrance.

I know Sydney's in there, and I know I want her. But for the first time since we met, doubt starts to creep into my mind. I'm questioning myself and wondering if the way I'm coming on so strongly is appropriate because she's right, the intensity with which I've pursued her is fucking crazy.

But that flicker of uncertainty lasts all of about five seconds.

Fuck it, I'm doing this my way.

The heavy scent of perfume and alcohol hits me as my eyes scan the crowded room, searching only for her, just like the first time I walked into the club.

Before I arrived, I had a conversation with Ash in which I insisted on spending time with Sydney again tonight, but without the cash offer—the girl had my fucking balls after I pulled that shit last time—to which he politely replied, "Go fuck yourself." He made it clear that she's one of his best and that he can't allow her to spend time away from the floor tonight, and as much as I want his head on a damn stick, I respect the way he runs his business.

I approach the bar, and a young woman with short red hair stands behind the counter, wiping down the glasses with a cloth. "Good evening, sir," she greets me with a friendly smile. "What can I get for you?"

"I'll take a whiskey, please," I say as my hands land flat on the bar. "And I'm looking for Sydney."

"She's dancing right now, but she should be done soon."

I fucking missed it.

After waiting restlessly for ten long minutes, I suddenly feel someone brush up against my arm. However, it's not Sydney. It isn't her scent, and after being so consumed by the smell of vanilla when she was in my car, there wasn't a chance I'd forget it. This floral fragrance coming from my left is definitely not hers.

I slowly turn my head and catch a glimpse of the beautiful woman standing beside me—and she is beautiful, but she's no match for the one I'm waiting for. Her chestnut hair cascades down her chest in tight curls that bounce with her every move. She's dressed in a mint-green two-piece set with matching stockings. It's not really my thing, but judging by the stares she's receiving from the men in the room, I'm clearly in the minority.

"You must be new here," she says, flashing a flirtatious smile.

"You could say that."

"Is there anything I can do for you? I can take you to one of our private rooms or join you for a drink if you want."

"I'm good, thanks," I answer abruptly, trying to hide my growing irritation, but she persists, and I can feel my patience wearing thin fast.

"Trust me, men don't come here to be alone."

"I'm actually waiting for someone, and the last thing I want is to be seen with another woman, but thank you for the offer."

"I'm sure she wouldn't mind if I kept you company." I can't help but roll my eyes internally as I lift my drink to my lips.

"I don't want to be rude, but I feel like you're not taking the hint," I snap without even turning to face her. "I'm not here for you, sweetheart. Now, please leave me alone and go do your job with somebody else."

I look up, and her cheeks turn a deep shade of red, a mix of anger and embarrassment. She regains her composure quickly, forcing a smile onto her lips as she walks away, her heels clicking loudly on the marble floor.

"I see you're making friends with the girls here," a silky voice murmurs from behind me.

My lips curl into a smile before I turn my head to face Sydney, and my breath catches in my throat when I see her dressed in a black-and-gold skirt—if you can even call it that—paired with a black bra that has the perfect swell of her breasts begging for my tongue.

"You look nice."

"Nice?" she asks, raising an eyebrow.

I take a moment to let my eyes linger on her, shamelessly drinking in every inch of her. "What would you like me to say?"

"Nothing you don't mean."

"Okay, you look like I want to sit you on top of this bar; slide whatever you're wearing under this skirt to the side so I can eat your pussy in front of every other asshole here who thinks he has any kind of shot with you."

My fingers toy with the hem of her skirt, feeling the soft fabric between my fingers as I push the club's 'no touching' boundary a little further. Her breasts rise and fall, commanding my attention once more, and this pull—this crazy lust-fueled chemistry—is on the verge of shattering at any moment.

"So you think I look nice, huh?"

"Something like that," I say as she draws a smile out of me. "Are you ready to let me take you to dinner yet?"

"I can't. I'm working"

"I swear to god, Sydney, say that to me one more time." I let out a low growl as she sets her hands on her waist, drawing my eyes to the dip of her curves. "Tomorrow night, and before you even try to argue, I already know you're not working."

"Of course you do."

"Is it really going to kill you to give me a few hours of your time?"

"Well, that depends. Will you be making a move on the waitress before I've had a chance to start my appetizer?"

Touché.

"No, but I never went on a date to Cora's with the intention of finding you."

"You realize you're not really selling this to me right now, don't you?"

"I sold it to you before my tongue was even in your mouth, baby."

"Could you be more arrogant?" she snaps as her gaze narrows on me.

I can feel her fiery side sparking to life, and I'm more than ready for it. I know she's going to push back, and I'd be lying if I said I didn't get off on the shit she likes to throw at me.

"It's the truth, and you're just being stubborn now." She steps closer, and our eyes connect as she settles between my legs. She's so close now—close enough that I could reach out and wrap my hand around her throat and drag her mouth to mine. But instead, she reaches for the glass of whisky in my hand, her fingers brushing against mine as she lifts the glass to her lips and drinks the last of it.

"To show you I'm not stubborn, I'll consider dinner, but it'll most probably be a no." She takes a step back and turns to walk away, leaving me with nothing but the sight of her perfect ass—an ass I'm desperate to mark, given how much she's testing me.

I watch Sydney closely as she moves through the room; she's impossible to ignore. She brushes several men's arms with a light touch, smiling sweetly at them, but with a seductive glimmer in her eyes.

She knows how to play this game.

Actually, it's more like she knows how to play them, how to lure them in without ever giving herself over.

And thank God because if I see anyone trying to get in the way of what I want my fists are gonna fly.

I'm not the type of guy who shares his girl, but I am the guy who will fuck her in front of you, and if her screaming my name when she comes isn't enough, then I'll fill her, claim her, and embed myself so deeply inside her until there's no doubt about who she belongs to.

Not that Sydney's my girl... yet.

Twenty-seven torturous minutes have passed, each one dragging out longer than the last. Jealousy burns in my throat, and I'm so fucking done watching her put her hands on men who aren't me.

Patience has never been my strong suit, and it's becoming increasingly clear as every second ticks away. Growing restless, I push myself up from the stool I've been sitting in all night and stride toward her. She's in the middle of a conversation with a short, balding man wearing a gold band on his wedding finger, which is laughable considering the way he's openly glaring at Sydney's body like he's ready to file for divorce.

Without a second thought, I reach out and wrap my arm possessively around her waist, spinning her and drawing her close to me. The voices and music around us fade into the background as we stand chest-to-chest, locked in our own private moment, while people move around, unaware of the tension pulsing between us.

"You're done with him, and I need a room with you right now, so tell me how I can make that happen."

"First of all, no touching," she says firmly. "Secondly, I can take you if it stops you from causing a scene." I release her and impatiently extend my arm, gesturing for her to take the lead.

My heart is pounding in my chest—fuck knows why—as she leads me down a hallway lit up by dim purple lights, and every dark and dirty fantasy I've ever had consumes my thoughts.

We stop in front of a door labeled *Lilac Doves*, and I watch as she punches in a code to open the room. As soon as the door clicks shut behind us, our bodies collide, and I have her pinned against it, my hands splayed on either side of her face.

My eyes zero in on her lips, taunting me with the way they part, like they're daring me to take what I want.

"Why are you fighting this?" The words come out rough, more a demand than a question, as I press my body close to hers.

"You can't touch me in here," she says, and I'm pretty sure she's deliberately trying to piss me off.

I trail my nose along her jaw, letting it rest at the curve of her neck, breathing in her scent. "You've been touching different men all night," I murmur, my voice edged with jealousy that I don't even try to hide.

"I'm free to touch whoever I want. It doesn't work both ways, and the rules are there for a reason, Mr. Miller."

"You haven't touched me once."

"Does that bother you?"

"You could say that."

"Ask yourself why I'm not touching you."

"Because you're trying to fuck with me, and believe me, baby, whatever you're doing is working." My voice is edged with the frustration that's been building up inside me all night. "You think I don't see what you're doing?" I whisper, my lips barely grazing the skin on her neck, "You're trying to make me lose my damn mind."

"No," she says, as her hands glide over my arms.

I've never hated wearing a jacket more—every inch of fabric feels like torture when all I want is her fingertips on my skin.

"It's because I actually want to touch you."

"Make it make sense before I say, fuck the damn rules."

"When I touch you, Edison, it'll be because I want to, not because I'm in a place where I'm being paid to."

"You said when, not if."

"I did."

"So you'll let me take you out?" She nods, and it's the only permission I need to get closer. I lean in, my lips brushing against her ear, desperate for another taste of her. "You do realize that these are my security cameras, right? I can log into the system and wipe it the second I leave this room."

"No need," she whispers. "The rules in this room are mine and mine alone, and in reality, we can do whatever the hell we want."

I can't even look at her without wanting to kiss her, and the way she's gazing up at me—so innocent yet so goddamn thirsty—tells me she knows it.

I grasp the back of her head, my fingers tangling in her hair as I slam my mouth against hers. She doesn't fight it. Instead, her hands curl into my jacket, pulling me closer, her body arching against mine as if she's been waiting for this.

I push my knee between her legs, nudging them apart, pressing against her just enough so she can feel exactly where my cock wants to be.

Our moans blend together, the kiss deepening as our tongues clash, each fighting for dominance, neither willing to back down. The taste of her drives me, and when I press my thigh against her core, I swallow the soft cry that escapes her.

Her body softens into mine, and yet, somehow, it's not enough—I find myself wanting more.

More of her mouth.

More of her cunt, which is currently soaking my thigh.

More of her attitude that turns me on just as much as it gives me a fucking headache.

Just more of her.

Reluctantly, I tear myself away from her mouth before I lose any last semblance of control and take her against the door without giving a single fuck about who might be watching.

"Get out," she says.

Suppressing a growl, I bite down on my lower lip before capturing her mouth in another kiss that causes my cock to harden to the point where it's almost painful.

"Get out before I find out if you can live up to that big dick energy."

"Trust me, baby, I'm good for it."

"I guess I'll have to take your word for it."

"For now," I say, watching as she shakes her head with a gentle laugh. "I'll send you a message when I leave my house tomorrow night."

"Because you came across my phone number when you figured out where I worked?"

"Precisely."

"And yet you haven't used it."

"It's pretty cute that you've been waiting on me, baby."

"I wasn't, but I assumed you were more persistent."

"I'm here now, aren't I?"

"Yeah, and I need you to go." With one last lingering kiss, I force myself to pull away and walk out the door, allowing every detail of my time with her to engrave itself into my memory—the way my body pressed against hers, the look in her eyes—I burn it all into my mind.

Chapter 5

Sydney

I'm back at the coffee shop, half-heartedly helping Cora with the morning rush, but my mind is anywhere but here. I try to focus on grinding beans, foaming milk, anything—yet the memories of last night keep slipping through the cracks.

Edison's kiss was a paradox—possessive and demanding yet somehow achingly tender, as if he were searching for something deeper. He kissed me like he wanted to crawl inside me, devouring me like he couldn't get close enough. Every sweep of his tongue felt like he was trying to drown himself in our connection, like I was the only thing that could satisfy the hunger burning inside him.

Last night, I left the club with the taste of him in my mouth and the smell of him on my skin that I washed away in the shower when I came with his name on my lips.

When Cora asks me why I'm smiling so hard, I spill every single detail. I tell her everything, and as I relive it, excitement settles in my stomach. Admittedly, I don't know why I'm not doing anything to discourage Edison when every logical part of me says I should, but there's just something about him that makes me unable to resist.

"I can't believe he's been to the club twice now. I told you he was into you, didn't I?" Cora says, her voice laced with that *I knew it* confidence.

Being a Virgo, she can't help but allow a smug little smile to spread across her beautiful face, knowing she was right all along.

"You don't think this is weird?"

"Weird?"

"You realize how fast this is moving isn't normal, right?" I blurt out, hoping she'll snap me out of this Edison fog and talk some sense into me because this whole situation is insane.

Cora's eyes narrow a little, and her smile fades. I want her to remind me of all the red flags, but she knows me well enough that all it will take is the slightest nudge, and I'll run in the opposite direction.

"So, you've kissed him twice," she states. "So what?"

"Okay, there's kissing and then there's this," I say as I return to cleaning the coffee machine. "This is next-level kissing that really has no right showing up until, I don't know, date four."

"Yeah, okay, so it's a little intense, but the guy obviously knows what he wants, and if you weren't equally into it, I know you'd have shut it down already."

I shrug and let out a sigh. "We'll see what happens tonight, I guess."

"You still think he's a fuckboy?" she asks.

"More like fuckman, but yeah, without a doubt."

"Because of what he did the day he came in here?" I nod as Cora removes the cloth from my hand and replaces it with a warm mug.

I take a sip of the cinnamon latte that she's been whipping up for me. Marshmallows melt on my tongue, and the red and green sprinkles, combined with the candy cane sticking out of it, make it feel like Christmas in a mug.

"Have you thought that maybe he's just a guy who knows what he wants and what he doesn't?"

"Or maybe he isn't used to rejection and believes he has something to prove to himself."

"I guess a man who looks the way he does must have some kind of ego," she replies, and she's right. Edison's confidence is undeniable, almost overwhelming, but it's that same confidence that keeps pulling me in. "Do you know where he's taking you?"

"All I know is he's picking me up from my apartment at eight o'clock."

"I'm telling you, girl, if you don't come in here tomorrow and tell me that you rode him to the moon and back, I'm firing you."

"I hardly know him."

She stops what she's doing, sets down the cloth she took from me, and turns to face me. Her brow furrows, and I know this look—it's the sympathy face that I saw every day after my breakup with Charlie.

"Listen, I know you've been hurt before with what that stupid shithead did to you, but not all men are like him." She pauses, but then the look disappears, and her smile is back. "There are some good ones out there."

"There's only one good one, and he's married now."

"Chris Evans?"

"He was it for me, and now he's gone."

"Okay, so you're not going to spend the rest of your life with America's ass, but Edison has a great ass too."

"My mom always taught me never to settle," I say with a smile, and we laugh as her arm wraps around my shoulder, and I rest my head against hers.

"Just give him a chance. Besides, Christmas is around the corner, and there's nothing wrong with spending it with someone who might actually buy you a really nice gift."

"I don't need a guy because I have you, and you get the best gifts."

"Don't give me that crap. Stop fighting the attraction and just go with it. What's the worst that can happen?" she asks, and a single thought races through my mind.

He'll get too close, then I'll get too close, and I'll be the one left broken when it all goes to shit.

Just as I'm about to respond, the coffee shop door swings open, and Nick, the guy who always delivers our supplies, walks in. He strides over to the counter, looking as handsome as ever.

Golden hair sweeps across his forehead, complementing the light stubble that lines his jaw, and as soon as he sees Cora, the smile he saves for her appears on his face.

I greet Nick with a simple "Hey," and he gives me a sweet smile before turning his attention right back to Cora. I've told her countless times that he likes her, but she never believes me. It doesn't help that for someone as attractive as Nick, he's surprisingly shy. He's got this quiet, understated confidence, but when it comes to Cora, it's like he's waiting for the perfect moment to make his move. I swear it's going to take a miracle for something to happen between them. But watching him now and seeing how he looks at her, I can't help but root for the guy and think maybe he just needs a little push.

"There isn't much here for you today," he says, carefully setting a couple of boxes on the counter. "Do you want me to carry these out back for you?"

"No, thank you. It's all staying on this side of the shop today." Nick nods, casually slipping his hands into his pockets. "Would you like something to drink? It's pretty cold out there."

"I'd appreciate a coffee," he says, and Cora offers him a smile as she starts to prepare his drink.

Nick leans against the counter, his eyes following her every move with an unmistakable look of adoration. A small smile tugs at my lips as I watch him, his eyes soft like he would happily stand there all day if it meant he could be near her.

"Are you sure that you don't want one of these?" I tease, raising my festive mug, and he laughs as he straightens up. He slips his hands back in his pockets, trying to play it off, but the slight blush creeping up his cheeks tells me he knows I caught him staring.

"Coffee is fine."

I walk out from behind the counter and grab Nick by the arm, dragging him down to the other end of the shop while Cora heads out back to grab some sugar. When we stop, I place my hands on his broad shoulders.

"Just ask her out." His mouth opens as if to object, but I cut him off before he can say anything. "Before you even think about lying to my face, I suggest you remember that it's almost Christmas and not the season for bullshit." His mouth snaps shut, and he remains silent. "Besides, it's clear to see that you're halfway in love with her and have been for a while."

"Do you think she knows?" he whispers, nodding toward the direction of the counter.

"Oh god, no, she has no clue. I've told her you like her because, dude, you're not subtle, but she doesn't believe me, so if you want her, you gotta do something about it."

In that sense, Nick is the complete opposite of Edison. That man gives no fucks when it comes to going after what he wants.

"Do you think she'd say yes if I asked?"

"You'll never know if you don't, but I wouldn't be having this conversation with you if I thought she'd say no." I nudge Nick playfully,

HIS FOR CHRISTMAS

and we make our way back to the counter. Cora has already set his coffee and a donut in a clear bag on the side, ready for him to take away.

"Here you are." She smiles and points at the donut. "That was the last one with the custard inside, so you came in at the perfect time."

With a grateful nod, he picks up the coffee and donut, meeting my eyes briefly before turning back to Cora.

"I'll stop by again tomorrow or maybe later today," he says. His gaze flicks to mine once more, and I give him an encouraging smile. "I'd like to talk to you about something," he adds softly, earning a smile from Cora.

"I'll be here," she replies.

We watch him as he walks away, and I patiently wait for Cora to stop staring after him before she turns to face me.

"What?" she asks, as if she hasn't just been caught drooling over the blond she's been crushing on since the first time she met him.

"Nothing," I say with a smile as I raise my drink to my lips to take the last sip of my Christmas hug in a mug.

After a long, hot shower, I wrap myself in a towel and step into my closet. My fingers trail over the hangers before settling on a black dress with a daring side split that climbs all the way up to my hip.

Butterflies start to swirl in my stomach, and I can't figure out why I'm so nervous all of a sudden. I've been on plenty of dates—although not so much recently—and worn plenty of dresses, but there's something about tonight that sets me on edge.

I haven't dated in a while, mainly because my previous relationship ended with me on the verge of chopping off my boyfriend's balls with some nail scissors. Plus, in my area of work, I see how loyalty and love are no longer valued, especially by disgustingly wealthy men who think they can do whatever and whoever they want based on the size of their bank accounts.

I know it seems like I hate all men—I get it—but I really don't.

I actually love men.

However, I'm also aware that they can take the form of human-shaped drugs—addictive, seductive, and the detox is a rip-your-heart-out kind of painful.

Maybe I'm a hypocrite.

Maybe I shouldn't be in the job I am when these thoughts plague my mind night after night, but a girl has to eat, and besides, I would never cross a line with anyone who enters that club.

Edison is different. He's unlike anyone I've ever met. Something about him draws me in beyond the physical attraction, which only makes me uncomfortable because I automatically want to build a wall around my already guarded heart. My instinct is to retreat, but it's like he's been thrown into my life by the universe just to challenge me and test how strong those walls really are.

After slipping on my heels, I make my way to the kitchen and grab a wine glass from the cabinet. I need something to calm these damn flutterings in my stomach.

I pour myself a large glass, but just as I set it down, my phone begins vibrating on the kitchen table, the screen lighting up with Edison's name.

"Hello."

"Hey, beautiful. You okay?" he says, his voice low and smooth, and damn it, the way he talks to me makes me feel giddy as fuck, and I can't help the smile that creeps onto my face.

"I'm fine. Are you? You sound stressed."

"I'm sorry, but something's come up at work, and I'll be a little later getting to you."

"That's fine, but if you get here and I don't come down, it's because I starved to death."

"Trust me, baby, I really don't want to be here. I'll get to you as quickly as I can."

The way he calls me baby like that ruins me.

"It's not a problem, honestly. I'll see you soon."

"I won't be long."

After ending the call, I walk into my living room and sink into my couch. I grab the remote and start flipping through channels, searching for some trash TV to distract me and pass the time.

Chapter 6

Edison

I've been thinking about tonight's date with Sydney all day. I've replayed how the night will unfold a hundred times—where we're going, the things I want to learn about her, how I'll keep a respectable distance when all I'm going to want is to be closer to her. Then there's the question of whether she's been thinking about it too, and I can't help but wonder if she's as wound up as I am.

I want to impress her and make her admit this attraction is more than just a passing spark—it's worth chasing.

But I'm not a diamonds and flowers guy. Never have been. All that shiny, romantic, surface-level stuff? It's nothing but superficial bullshit.

I'd rather show her something real, something that feels honest, even if it's not wrapped in a pretty bow.

From what I already know about Sydney, material things don't impress her. She hated that I paid to spend time with her, which probably wasn't my smartest move, but what's a guy to do when he's out of options?

If things go well between us and if, over time, I can break through her walls, I can promise her something real, something she won't be able to ignore. She'll become addicted to me in ways she never thought possible.

Every night I'll warm her bed, and I'll touch her in a way that'll make her ache for me until her body learns that the only one who can satisfy her is me.

As soon as I stepped through my front door last night, I kicked off my shoes and headed straight for the shower. The moment the water hit my skin, heat seeped into my muscles, easing the tension but doing absolutely nothing to quiet the memory of Sydney in that room. The bruising intensity of our kiss lingered like it was branded onto me, and every time it replayed in my mind, my body responded in a way I didn't even know a kiss could—*for the second time now.*

Needing a release, I frantically fucked my hand as I remembered the feeling of her lips on mine, the sweet taste of her mouth, and the heat that emanated from her body. All I wanted was to get her out of her clothes. I wanted her open and ready for me to get inside her. I didn't care if it was my fingers, tongue, or cock—I just needed to feel her in any way possible.

I know she's into me, even if she doesn't want to be. I see it in the way she looks at me and the way her gaze lingers. But I'd be stupid if I couldn't see that she's guarded.

She doesn't want to let me in or open herself up emotionally to me, and that's fine because we've only just met, but I swear to fuck, I'll hammer that wall down until it crumbles, leaving her with no choice but to show me every part of her.

There's something about her that drives an uncontrollable obsession within me. I don't believe in love at first sight—that isn't what this is—but I believe in connections, and I can't ignore this one.

How can you meet someone and feel completely out of sync with them when someone else's energy is so closely matched to yours that you may as well be bound to them?

Perched on the end of my bed, my towel clings to my damp skin. My phone starts ringing on the nightstand, and seeing Lee's name flash up on the screen only aggravates me.

I made it clear to my team that I wasn't to be disturbed tonight, so when I see him calling, I know there's a problem.

"What's wrong?" I ask as I answer the call.

"We've got a problem, Ed."

"Can it wait?"

"I don't think so."

I let out a frustrated sigh as I rub my jaw with my hand. "Jesus, what is it?"

"We've been made aware of a high-profile case today, but the client has decided to take matters into their own hands and is refusing to listen to me."

"Who is it?"

"It's Maddy."

Of course it is.

"What's happened?"

"She believes she's being stalked again and needs round-the-clock security, but she wants to meet with you to discuss it."

"Tell her she can wait until tomorrow."

"She insisted on coming to your house even though I told her you weren't free tonight."

Fuck my life.

"I need you and Clint to get your asses here as soon as we get off the phone. I'm not dealing with her alone."

"We'll get there as quickly as possible." I let out a frustrated groan before hanging up and running my fingers through my hair.

I glance at the clock, knowing I have an hour before I'm supposed to pick up Sydney, but I also know that my ex is going to make that impossible.

I slip into my clothes, fingers fumbling over buttons and zippers as I rush to get dressed. Grabbing my phone and laptop, I tuck them under my arm and sprint down the stairs, but before I reach the bottom step, a loud knock echoes through the house. I can't see through the frosted glass beside the door, but I know it's not Lee and Clint.

Opening the door, I see Maddy standing on the doorstep, dressed in a long red coat and oversized sunglasses, as if she's stepped straight out of a bad movie. "Nice outfit," I say dryly, my eyes narrowing at her.

She barges past me, colliding with my chest as she stumbles into the entryway. "Oh my god, I can't tell you how relieved I am to see you," she cries, throwing her arms around me. I gently tap her shoulder, denying her the embrace she's seeking because the urge to get as far away from her as possible dominates every other thought.

"How are you, Maddy?" I ask, and she dramatically sniffles against my chest. Her grip on me tightens, but my body remains rigid.

"I'm terrified, Edison," she says, her voice trembling with just enough emotion to sound convincing. But she's a fucking actress, and I don't trust a word that comes out of her mouth.

"You want a coffee?" I offer, gesturing toward the kitchen. She nods, removing her sunglasses and wiping her eyes of the tears that I doubt were ever there. Maddy walks ahead of me, heels clicking against the floor as she takes a seat at the kitchen island. "We're just waiting on Lee and Clint," I explain as I press a few buttons on my coffee machine.

"What do you mean? Why do we need them here?"

"Because this is business, Maddy, and I won't be around tonight. I need my guys to know what's going on so they can deal with the problem."

"So you're saying that you have somewhere more important to be than right here discussing my safety?"

I haven't seen her in over six months, and now she has the audacity to act shocked at my response, like she can't believe that I'm not dropping everything for her.

"If I had it my way, you wouldn't be here, and we wouldn't be having this conversation. But as usual, Maddy does what Maddy wants."

"I need your help, Edison," she begs.

I lean forward, pushing a steaming mug of coffee toward her. "What you need is what my company can offer you. Whether you like it or not, Lee is in charge now, and he personally ensures that the right men are assigned to each job."

"So what the hell do you do now?" she asks, her victim mask slipping slightly as her tone returns to the one I can't fucking stand and really haven't missed.

"Whatever I want."

"You're acting like we didn't spend almost a year together. I'm not just a client, Edison."

You ever wish you could go back in time and unmeet someone?

"Actually, that's all you are, and that's exactly how I'm going to treat you."

Our conversation is thankfully interrupted by a knock on the door, and I rush to open it. Lee's tall frame fills my doorway before he walks in, followed closely by Clint. They both shoot me an apologetic look, fully aware of the shitshow they're walking into, but right now, I'm just relieved that they're here.

Lee has been with me since I started Miller Security. He's like a younger brother to me, or as close to one as I'll ever have, which is why I've handed over the reins to him. He's younger than me, about to turn thirty-two, and he still possesses the hunger and drive to make his job his priority. Meanwhile, I've done the high-risk jobs and lived the playboy lifestyle, but it's not what I want anymore and hasn't been for a long time. All I want now is to live quietly with a woman I'm obsessed with and maybe have a few kids who will fill this place with noise and make this house a home.

I love the business I built; I'm damn proud of it. But there's got to be more to life than chasing the next contract.

I know there's more to life; I've seen it in my parents' love and the way they built a life together, and that's what I want now.

"Sorry about this, boss." Lee apologizes as he runs his fingers through his jet-black hair.

"It's fine, but I have to make a phone call. Maddy's in the kitchen."

Clint and Lee walk past me as I take out my phone to call Sydney. I brace myself, mentally preparing myself for her fiery attitude, but when she picks up, her voice is calm, surprising me with her understanding.

After hanging up, I slide my phone back into my pocket and return to the kitchen, where Maddy sits with her hands clasped around the mug in front of her.

She begins by recounting how it all started with handwritten letters being delivered to her doorstep, each signed with a strange signature she didn't recognize. Then came the deliveries of flowers. Initially, she received a single rose, but as the days went by, they began to arrive more damaged—petals torn off, stems bent—until all she received were the broken, decapitated stalks. Her voice wavers as she recounts every detail, telling us how the fear has taken over her life, and now she's living in a hotel, trying to escape someone who always seems to know exactly where she is.

An hour passes and she's still talking. As much as I try to stay attentive, I can feel my patience wearing thin.

My relationship with Maddy was toxic, and I didn't like the person I became when I was with her. She brought out the worst in me, something I will never allow to happen again, which is why I need to keep my distance from her—for the sake of my own mental health. Her mindfuckery left me with severe trust issues for a time, and it took months of self-reflection before I went back to being the man I was before I met her.

The gaslighting—that's what eventually broke me. She twisted everything, made me question my sanity, and manipulated the shit out of me. It took me watching a video of her sucking off the director from one of her movies for me to break out of the downward spiral she sent me into.

Ending the relationship was the best thing I ever did. It's been a couple of years now, but Maddy still tries to reach out and reconnect with me from time to time.

Once, and only once, since I was so disgusted with myself afterward, I made the mistake of meeting up with her in a bar, which led to me getting stupidly drunk, and I ended up in her apartment. I spent the night having the most vanilla sex with her, and once it was over, I was filled with regret.

Pretty sure I didn't come either.

I look at Maddy now and know I didn't care about her yesterday. Don't really give a fuck about her today, and despite her troubles, I sure as shit won't care about her tomorrow.

Maddy has a stalker, no doubt, but she's been down this road before. Luckily, the cops found the guy quite quickly last time, and after reading the police report, it's obvious that they'll be taking this just as seriously a second time around. Until they find out who the person is, I'm willing to provide her with the security she needs. I'm not heartless, and the last thing I want is for something to actually happen to her, but I need her to hurry the fuck up so I can get everyone out of here and get my ass to Sydney.

I let out a heavy sigh, running a hand through my hair as I glanced down at the watch on my wrist. "Are we done here?"

"We just need to find suitable accommodation for Miss Cander. She said she doesn't feel safe at her current location," Lee says, looking at me like he can smell bullshit from a mile away. He was there, watching everything I went through with her, and if there's anyone who hates Maddy more than I do, it's him.

"You're in a hotel, so what's the problem?" I ask.

"Everyone knows I'm there."

"How?" I snap.

"I was seen, and it spread all over social media."

People need to put down their phones and start living instead of taking photos of crazy women going in and out of hotels.

"I was thinking that maybe I could..." She trails off, looking at me as if she's waiting for me to step in like a goddamn hero and offer a solution that keeps her close, and it hits me what she's getting at.

She wants to stay here—with me.

Oh, hell no.

"No way. Not happening, Maddy," I say, my tone sharp as I turn to Clint. "Get started on finding her accommodation. I want this done within the next ten minutes." I storm out of the kitchen, bracing myself against the staircase.

I have my phone in my hand again, my thumb hovering over Sydney's name, and I already know I don't want to make this call. This is the last thing I wanted tonight—getting dragged into Maddy's mess when all I've been thinking about is finally spending some time getting to know the girl I've been obsessing over. It's completely unfair to Sydney. She shouldn't have had to have been put on hold tonight because of my past—a past that literally forced her way into my home.

If I say I'm going to do something, I do it, and yet I know I've let her down.

Chapter 7

Sydney

It's been an hour since Edison's call, and my girl brain is beginning to shut down all of my rational thoughts, edging me toward the wrong side of crazy.

Ignore the psycho bitch, Sydney. There's obviously been a problem, just like he said.

It's already nine o'clock, and my bed is calling out to me.

When I'm not at the club, I'm wrapped in the warmth of my bed by this time every night, sinking into a book or half-watching a movie with a hot drink in my hands.

Just as I'm contemplating heading into the kitchen to make a hot chocolate, my phone starts to ring, as if I just manifested it. When I press the green button, Edison begins to speak before I can even say hello.

"Sydney, I'm so sorry, but I'm still in this meeting."

A frown forms on my face as I try to push away the disappointment, a reaction I wasn't expecting, but the sinking feeling in my stomach confirms it.

"I'll be finishing up here soon. I can still make—"

"I think we should just put tonight on hold," I blurt out, interrupting him mid-sentence because, honestly, something's urging me to run in the opposite direction. "Maybe we could move it to when you're not so busy." There's a pause on his end, and the silence only makes my heart thud faster.

"Maybe?" he asks as if that word has no place in our conversation.

"Look, I understand that you're a busy guy."

"I want to do this, Sydney. Do you understand that?"

Just as I'm about to respond, I hear a woman's voice, light and teasing. *"Where's your wine, Edison? I need a glass before we head to the hotel."*

Well, I understood that.

A dry, bitter laugh slips from my lips. "Yeah, I'm gonna go," I say, already done with this whole situation.

"Sydney." He says my name firmly, attempting to reel me back in while I try my hardest to pull away.

But I'm all out of fucks to give.

"We don't need to do this. It was one date."

"A date I still want."

"Yeah, well, it sounds like you've got your hands full."

"It's not what you think."

"It's also not my business, and honestly, I don't really care. So please, just let it go, Edison." I don't wait for his response. I end the call, power off my phone, and toss it onto the couch, where it lands just shy of the remote.

I try to ignore the fact that he's a lying piece of shit who's been spending the night with another woman while feeding me all kinds of crap, but I'm pissed.

I'm even a little hurt.

Mostly, I just feel like an idiot.

Fix your shit, Sydney. You're not his girlfriend, so you have no right to care who or what he does.

God, why did he keep asking me out? Why be so persistent if he intended to make me wait all night while he sees another woman first? I will never understand men who get off on the chase, and then, as soon as you give a little, they're balls deep in someone else.

I don't care how attractive he is or how much his kisses weaken me to the point where I feel boneless. I have enough self-respect to know how I deserve to be treated.

After deciding against settling down with a hot drink, I opt for a bottle of red wine instead, needing something to take the edge off.

As I finish my second glass, there's a sudden knock at my door. Even though I want to believe it's someone else, anyone but that persistent asshole who can't take no for an answer, deep down I know it's him. I set my glass down on the coffee table, stand up, and smooth down my dress before making my way to the front door.

I slowly open it, and Edison's large hands tighten their grip on the frame's edges as if he's trying to hold himself back. His muscles ripple beneath his shirt, and the hint of a tattoo peeking out from the fabric draws my attention to his chest. When our eyes lock, my treacherous body can't help but respond to his. Our heavy breaths fill the small space between us, but there's a fire in his eyes, and I can't tell if it's fueled by anger or desire.

Maybe it's both.

"Let it go? Are you fucking serious?"

"Completely," I reply unflinchingly as I hold his gaze.

"Not happening, Sydney. Not when what you're thinking is so far from the truth." His voice drops lower, rougher, as his eyes travel down my body, drinking in every inch of me. As he settles on my dress, one of his hands drops from the doorframe to caress his jaw. "Is this what you wore for me tonight?"

"Not for you," I snap.

"Liar," he says, his hungry gaze tracing the curves of my body. "I know you think I'm an asshole right now, and I get it, but you look like I want to throw you into my sheets and never let you leave them."

The effect he has on me is frustrating as hell, and I would love for it to fuck right off.

"You look beautiful, Sydney."

"Thanks. You done?"

The muscles in his jaw are tense, as if he's holding back a million things that he wants to say, and a familiar look of frustration flickers across his face.

He's pissed. Good.

"Not even close," he growls, his steel-gray eyes darkening as they burn into mine. "Now I suggest you let me in because I'm not leaving until you get it in your head that the only woman I'm interested in is you, despite what you believe is going on here." His words cut through my defenses as he slowly lowers his hands from the doorframe and steps forward.

I reluctantly hold the door open wider for him, feeling like I'm letting the devil into my home as he confidently strides in, claiming the space between us as if it were his own.

Chapter 8
Edison

During our phone call, I could feel Sydney pulling away, placing more and more distance between us until she hung up on me. Frustration burned through me, and without a second thought, I kicked Maddy out of my house—no explanation, no apology.

Fortunately, Lee and Clint managed to find her somewhere to stay, but honestly, she could spend the night on the streets with her stalker, and I wouldn't give one single fuck at this point.

I drove to Sydney's apartment on pure impulse. By the time I got there, I was running on nothing but adrenaline, determined to make her understand that she's got this all wrong. She'd twisted everything in her mind, casting me as someone I'm not, and I wasn't about to let her keep believing it.

Not her. Not now.

When the door swung open, my breath caught in my throat, and I had to tighten my grip on the doorframe to keep myself from reaching for her.

How the hell would I have ever survived a night with her in this damn dress?

I'm so insanely attracted to her that I can feel myself going a little more crazy the longer I look at her.

I step into her apartment, but I quickly turn to face her, needing my eyes back on her like I need my next breath. She's wearing a tight black dress that clings to her body in all the right places, emphasizing every delicious curve with a split on the side that's teasing the hell out of me. My gaze follows the split as it rides higher up her thigh, exposing the most beautiful pair of legs I've ever seen.

She shuts the door behind me, and I pause for a moment to fully appreciate just how beautiful she is—the kind of beauty that steals your focus and makes your body ache.

"You've got five minutes, Edison."

"Why? You going somewhere?" I try to lighten the mood between us, but it backfires instantly. The anger etched on her face suggests that my attempt at humor was a huge fucking error.

"This isn't cute, and I'm not playing this game, so say what you need to and leave."

"Look, I'm sorry about tonight, okay? What happened was out of my control, and I would appreciate it if you could give me a chance to make it up to you."

"I feel like I made myself clear on the phone."

"You've got shit mixed up here, baby. I'm not that guy." She laughs—that same one she gave me when she heard Maddy's voice on the phone.

"Seriously? Have you forgotten how we met?" she fires back, her words hitting me like a slap, and maybe I deserve it, but it pisses me off that she's placing me in a box I don't belong in.

"I've already explained that to you. I'm not going to do it again."

"I'm not asking you to, and you're free to leave if you don't like where this conversation is going."

Keep pushing me, baby, but I'll keep pushing back.

"What happened tonight was work—nothing more. I can't go into detail, which I'm sure you understand, but I promise it's not what you're thinking."

She locks her gaze on mine, her green eyes darkening like a forest in the fading sunlight rather than their usual light-emerald color.

"It's really none of my business. Now, I won't lose any sleep over this, so if you're done." She gestures toward the door, making it clear that she's finished with this conversation, and with every breath I take, I can feel my control slipping away.

"I'm not fucking done, Sydney," I practically shout as she stands there, tearing me apart with her eyes and completely dismissing me.

"Well, I am," she replies calmly, but I hear a slight shake in her voice.

Her walls are fully up when it comes to me, but I'm going to have so much fun tearing them all down.

"Bullshit. You're about as done as I am, which is nowhere fucking near."

"Do you know how much I hate guys like you?"

"I'm not like them."

"No, you're worse because you really sold it, and like a dumbass, I bought it."

"Sydney..."

"Lose my number and stay the hell away from the club."

My eyes burn into hers, and in a sudden uncontrollable rush of need, I slam her against the wall, pinning her as my body presses into hers. My lips hover beside her ear, my breath hot against her skin as I murmur, low and possessive, "Fuck. That."

I crush my mouth against hers, gripping her wrists and pinning them above her head, claiming her with a rawness that feels as unstoppable as it is intense. I pull back for a breath, and she tilts her head, defiant fire blazing in those green eyes as she holds my gaze, daring me. "Open your mouth," I command, my voice thick with need. Her lips part, and I plunge my tongue inside, feeding off the heat between us.

What is it about this girl that I can't get enough of?

For starters, nothing about her is predictable, and the chaos adds to the attraction.

I release her wrists, my hands trembling as I drag my fingers down her exposed thigh before wrapping it around my waist. I press my body against hers, grinding my painfully hard cock against her center until she lets out a whimper, and I pull back, looking down at her. My gaze falls to her swollen lips, and as our eyes meet again, it's clear that she craves me just as badly as I crave her.

My hips thrust forward, grinding her harder against the wall as I dry-hump the fuck out of her. "You feel that, baby? It's all you. Every inch of me is aching for you." I growl into her ear as she lets out a small, breathy cry. "From the moment I saw you, all I've wanted to do is bury my cock inside you, and god, I can't wait to feel how tight and wet you are, but it won't be tonight, and it won't be like this."

I run my thumb along her cheek, letting my hand trail down to rest at the curve of her throat as I lean in, my words slipping softly over her lips.

"You're pissed at me right now, and I get it. I understand why." My thumb brushes against the pulse point in her neck, feeling the rapid beat of her heart matching mine. I glide my fingers down her neck, tracing the outline of her collarbone before moving lower to graze her nipple through the thin fabric of her dress. "But the first time I slide into your pussy, your mind will want it just as much as your body does." My hand lowers, knuckles brushing against the soft skin of her thigh. "Not like this, though, Sydney. Not when you believe I've done something I haven't and that I'm someone I'm not."

She lifts her chin defiantly, her eyes narrowing as they focus on my mouth. "Then you'll never be inside me."

This girl and her stubbornness are going to kill me.

As she taunts me, my fingers inch closer to the edge of her panties. "You're that sure you know me?" I ask, knowing that in a few seconds, I'll finally get to feel the warmth of her cunt.

"You're no different from the guys who pay for my time, while their wives..." Her voice falters, cut off by a sharp intake of breath as my fingers now brush against the front of her underwear.

Her eyes flutter shut as she continues to fight this losing battle, but I know this thing between us is consuming her as much as it is me.

"I wouldn't finish that sentence if I were you, beautiful," I warn as my fingers drift lower between her thighs. "Besides, if you really believed that, Sydney..." I ghost my lips against hers while my fingers trace gentle circles over her lace panties, my other hand gripping the base of her throat once again. "Then your body wouldn't ache for me, and your underwear wouldn't be soaked."

I keep her pinned against the wall, my mouth lowering to suck her nipple through her dress. "If you want me to stop touching you, then say the fucking word, or I'm going to make you come all over my fingers." She tightens her grip on my wrist, pressing it harder into her throat while silently begging for more with her eyes alone.

I can see the struggle within her, torn between wanting to be controlled and resisting it. She wants to experience that loss of control, the release that comes with letting go, with being taken. But she also fights it, afraid to give herself over completely, like she's scared of what it means to trust someone with her vulnerability.

However, when I have her in my grip like this, I'm more than happy to possess her and give her the one thing she wants but will never ask for or admit she needs.

She's tense beneath me, but her hips move in rhythm with my fingers, and her breaths grow more desperate.

"It's okay to want this, Sydney," I whisper, my lips brushing against her jaw as I tease her over her underwear. "Let me give you what you need, or do you want me to stop?"

"Don't you dare stop," she gasps as my hand slides into the front of her underwear.

"You get off on calling me out on my shit, baby? Because your pussy is dripping." I thrust a finger inside her, then another, and her back arches away from the wall. "So soft. So fucking tight."

I press the heel of my palm against her clit while my fingers work inside her, and her hips buck against my hand. "Fuck, yes. Oh god," she moans, her voice catching between breaths.

"Come on, baby. Make a mess on my fucking hand."

I watch her unravel, completely hooked on the sight of her losing herself as she starts to shake in my hold. She clenches around my fingers as they work in and out of her, curling and pressing in just the right way.

Her eyes are shut, lips parted with a breathless moan, and the way she's baring herself to me, dropping those walls, and giving me a piece of her is something I commit to memory, knowing that this might be the closest she ever lets me get.

"Keep going," she whispers, grinding harder, her nails digging into my arm, leaving crescent marks on my skin. I release my hold on her throat, running my tongue along her neck before sucking on her skin and leaving my own mark that'll guarantee she remembers this tomorrow. "Edison... don't stop," she breathes, my name spilling from her lips with an edge that shoots straight to my dick, making it ache to be inside her.

"Open your eyes and look at me, Sydney," I demand, and her lashes flutter before locking those piercing green eyes on mine. A cry escapes her lips as her orgasm crests, and she starts to come, her wetness coating my hand. "That's it, baby. That's my girl," I praise, my cock throbbing as it presses against my pants.

I wonder if she realizes she has the power to bring me to my knees and give me something to pray for or, at the very least, beg for.

I gently drag my nose across her jaw, inhaling the subtle hint of vanilla that clings to her skin. Her body trembles beneath me, still caught in the aftershocks of her release, each shallow breath a reminder of the pleasure that just tore through her.

"My fingers just made your entire body shake, Sydney. Now imagine what my tongue can do." I lick across her lower lip before I kiss the hell out of her, claiming her mouth as I slide out of her. I bring my fingers to my lips, sucking her arousal away and holding her eyes, deepening this connection between us.

She's the goddamn storm I could go crazy for—the way she challenges me, the way she submits to me.

"Has anyone ever told you how beautiful you look when you come?" She laughs, and I already know it's going to be one of my favorite sounds. "We're going to try this again tomorrow night, okay? And I swear, nothing will stop me from being here to pick you up." Her eyes search for any hint of deception, and I get it—I haven't been completely honest with her yet.

"One chance, Edison. If you're not here, there won't be another."

"I only need one." She nods—just the slightest tilt of her chin, but it's enough.

We stand there for long seconds, staring into each other's eyes, and my body literally aches as I struggle to resist this urge to sink my cock inside her. My dick is raging and hates me for refusing to fuck her, but while she believes there's a chance I was with somebody else tonight, there's no way I'm giving in to this need. If I have to leave here hard as a rock to prove my point, then so be it—but damn if I won't be getting my ass home and fucking my fist the second I step inside my house, replaying every moment of her coming undone in my hands.

"I'm going before I don't go."

"Okay," she replies, giving me the bare minimum.

"I'll pick you up at eight." She nods, but that uncertain expression still lingers on her face.

I move toward the front door, slowly opening it while making sure that I keep a safe distance from her because fuck me, walking away when I'm this tightly wound is almost impossible. But I push through it, and before I leave, I allow myself one last glance at her—she's still flushed, looking freshly fucked and so goddamn tempting.

Chapter 9
Sydney

I've never considered myself submissive. I've always prided myself on being a strong, independent woman. I have no tolerance for bullshit and can hold my own in any situation. But as Edison pressed his body against mine and whispered dirty words in my ear, he had me completely under his control. I was at his mercy, and if he had asked, I would've begged.

The tension between us snapped, and so did my brain, apparently. Logic and reason no longer existed, and all that was left was a raw, aching need to be whatever he needed. I was prepared to do anything he wanted, even if it meant getting down on my knees and calling him Daddy.

Daddy Edison does have a ring to it.

No way. I can't pull that off. Besides, I've never said the word "Daddy" in my entire life.

Edison's touch was unlike anything I had ever felt, and now that I've had a taste, I want more.

Despite every instinct screaming at me not to believe him, there's a part of me that wants to trust what he told me last night.

Yet, for reasons I can't quite justify—even to myself—I'm convinced Edison needs a lesson after what happened before he showed up at my apartment. Call it petty, but I want to make him squirm a little. He needs to realize I'm not a doormat, and if a bit of pushback is what it takes to get that message across, then so be it.

Maybe it's a little cruel, but I've been burned before, and I value my heart way too much to let another guy shatter it.

Never again.

Not after witnessing the most broken version of myself, which took too long to heal.

I need him to understand that I won't be the type of woman who waits around for him while he's off with other women and who obeys his every command—except when it comes to sex, apparently, seeing as my vagina decided to be a slut and betray me.

He found a weakness I didn't even know I had, and he didn't think twice about exploiting it. What's worse is that I didn't even make a single attempt to stop him. I lost myself in him, and every ounce of control I thought I had slipped through my fingers like water.

My closet is hands down the thing I love most about my apartment—I channeled my inner Carrie Bradshaw when I was looking for a place, and it's perfect. It's a walk-in dream with shelves full of clothes and shoes, and a full-length mirror stands proudly in the center. Right now, the whole room is lit up like a Christmas tree because, well, it's December, and I thought, why the hell not?

I slip into a strapless white dress that molds to my curves like it was custom-made. The color radiates purity, but the way it clings to me hints at the promise of sins waiting to be unleashed. With a neckline that dips low enough to tease, I finish the look with a few pieces of sparkling silver jewelry.

Innocence wrapped in temptation—that's the look I'm going for.

Something that tells Edison he can't be too mad at me but, at the same time, makes him want to rage-fuck me for seeing how far I could push him tonight.

Even with the mess from last night still fresh in my mind, I'm feeling confident, but also a little like Edison is going to hand me my ass when he eventually finds me.

I step into my living room, pick up my phone from the coffee table, and fire off a quick message to the man who won't leave my mind.

> S: Hey, I would've called, but I know you're a busy guy. Something's come up, and I can't make it tonight. Talk soon.

Either he'll really let it go this time, or he'll come searching for me. And if he does, I already know I'm his for the night.

I've been sitting alone at the bar in The Dancing Lilacs for twenty minutes now. My nails tap nervously against the cool glass in my hand as I keep my eyes fixed on the door, scanning the familiar faces of everyone who walks in. I came here because I didn't want to make it impossible for him to find me. If he decides to look for me, then making it hard on purpose would just be mean.

I check the time on my phone, seeing that it's just past eight o'clock. Four missed calls from Edison stare up at me, and a pang of guilt twists in my gut. I know that if the roles were reversed, I'd be ready to commit murder for being ignored like this.

I'm not officially working tonight, but I play my part while I'm here, slipping effortlessly into the role I mastered a long time ago.

I've been especially welcoming and complimentary to the little men in the room, ensuring that I feed their fragile egos despite not being paid to.

"Well, aren't you equally stunning in and out of clothing?" That smooth voice catches my attention, and when I turn on my barstool, I look up at Huxley Foster—son of Hollywood director Caleb—towering over me.

"Thanks, Huxley."

Go fuck yourself, Huxley.

His golden hair is perfectly styled, every strand meticulously placed like he just stepped off the cover of a magazine. There's no denying that Huxley is attractive in that rich overconfident way that assholes like him always are. He's got that chiseled jaw and piercing blue eyes that scream privilege, but I found out very quickly that he's an entitled little brat with unresolved daddy issues.

The guy makes my skin crawl.

Huxley Foster believes that because he's hot and his dad regularly works with Tom Cruise, he has a free pass to do whatever the hell he wants. Flirting is one thing, but Huxley constantly crosses the line, getting handsy with the girls here despite the strict no-touching rule. Clearly, he has no concept of boundaries and acts like the word "no" doesn't apply to him.

It's fucking infuriating.

However, Ash won't intervene until there's a formal complaint, and I get it; nobody wants to poke the beast when said beast is the son of a five-time Oscar-winning director who allegedly holds a lot of influence in a way that would send you down a rabbit hole if you tried to look into it.

"How much would it cost me to get you out of this dress for the night?" Huxley whispers into my ear.

Too fucking close.

"I'm not working tonight, and even if I was, I'm not paid by clients. That's not how this works, and you know it," I say firmly as I glare up at him.

"Good, because I like the idea of getting you for nothing."

This situation is relatively mild for this douchebag. Give him a couple of hours and more alcohol than he should be allowed, and he'll be leaning in too close, slurring out all the ways he thinks he could make me come. The last time he approached me, he used the words "squeal like a pig," a phrase that likely earns him a one-way ticket to rejection in real life.

But then a lot of the men here have no filter and lack basic respect when it comes to speaking to women—or maybe it's just the ones who work here.

You have to be able to handle yourself in this environment.

You have to ignore the vulgar comments and the way these smug bastards look at you like they already own you because if you show any sign of weakness, you'll never survive the night.

"I'm actually waiting for someone, Huxley, so you'll need to find one of the other girls to spend the evening with."

"Come on, it's almost Christmas," he says, stepping closer to me, standing tall as his hand clamps down on my arm.

The sharp scent of his cologne hits me, suffocating me, and my body tenses because *what in the fucking audacity?* He only ever put his hands on me once before, and I threatened to smash his jewels into powder.

"You can't just dangle yourself in front of me like some forbidden fruit, Sydney," he growls, leaning in until his face is mere inches from mine, his hot breath hitting my skin.

"Take your hand off me." My voice shakes with rage as I spit out the words through gritted teeth, but he only smiles.

"Hey, asshole, she told you to take your hands off her." A deep, threatening voice cuts through the air. "And if you don't do it in the next two seconds, I'll have you on the ground with your jaw ripped from your face."

Anxiety, relief, excitement—fucking butterflies all hit me at once when I hear Edison's voice from behind me.

I watch Huxley's face twist in confusion, his eyes widening as he takes in Edison's full height. "Who the hell are you?" he stutters as his hand withdraws from my body.

"I'm the guy who gets to touch her all night. Now fuck off before I show you what happens when you put your hands on a woman who doesn't want them there." Huxley's lips curl into a sneer as he turns and walks away, his face red from embarrassment.

Edison positions himself in front of me, his eyes like steel blades that slice through me, and for a second, I forget how to breathe.

For the first time, I'm seeing him in something that isn't a suit. His jacket hugs his broad shoulders, and the black T-shirt beneath clings to every muscle—he's dripping in sex and something else.

It's anger. He's mad at me.

"You want to explain to me what the hell you're doing here?" he says calmly. But he's anything but calm; there's a dangerous edge to his tone, and I can't help but derive some twisted pleasure from it.

"Not really."

"No?" he asks, his voice laced with fury.

I can see it simmering behind his unfairly beautiful eyes—eyes that could promise heaven as easily as they could threaten hell.

"No, now let's go," I say as I rise and pick up my purse from the bar.

"What?"

I close the distance between us, pressing my body into his, and reach up on my toes. My heels add a few inches to my height, allowing my lips to graze the sensitive shell of his ear as I breathe him in, and the scent of cedar and sandalwood overwhelms me.

It's raw masculinity, and it's all him.

"You can be mad because I fucked you around tonight, or you can take me out and then bring me home and do every dirty thing you've been imagining." As I pull back, his chest rises and falls rapidly before he finally speaks, his eyes darkening as they focus on me.

"You don't know what you're asking for, baby, because right now, all I wanna do is punish your ass."

"Trust me. I know exactly what I'm asking for." He drags his hand across his jaw before firmly grasping my wrist and guiding me out of the club.

Now, I know nothing about cars, but as we approach a matte-black sports car, I can tell it's worth a fortune—probably more than I make in a year.

Suddenly, the cool metal of the car presses against my back, and his muscular thigh slides between my legs, sending a rush of heat to my core. His large, tattooed hands cup my face, urging me to meet his gaze.

He teasingly hovers his lips close to mine, and all I can think about is how badly I need him to kiss me.

"Nothing is going to happen between us until I have this date with you. Do you understand?"

"You don't wanna touch me, Edison?" I whisper his name, and a lust-filled groan escapes his lips.

"Don't fuck with me, Sydney. I've already had enough of your shit tonight." His thumb brushes my cheek—a small act of tenderness amidst the tension between us. "Let me get to know you. Let me in."

Of all the things I was expecting him to say, that wasn't it, and I can't help but feel some of my defenses crumble away.

"Because as badly as I want you to let me in here..." He pushes his thigh harder against my center, and my body shudders. "What I really want is for you to let me in here," he murmurs as he caresses my temple with his thumb.

"Why?" I ask, my voice shaking slightly as I stare back at him.

"You wanna know why I'm not just trying to get into your pants?" He laughs, so deep and throaty, while a playful spark dances in his eyes. All I can do is nod, and I realize I've unintentionally revealed a glimpse of myself and my vulnerability. "Because I kinda like your crazy ass, and I want to know more about you."

"Ah, okay, so you like punishing yourself?" I ask with a playful grin.

"Not nearly as much as I'd like to punish you, baby."

The chemistry between us is too strong to ignore, drawing my eyes to his mouth. But instead of giving in to this, he reaches behind me, his fingers brushing my back as he opens the car door.

"Ready to go?" he asks as he climbs in beside me.

"Are you?"

"No, not really. But we're doing this."

I'm hot as hell right now. I feel like I'm about to combust, unable to tear my eyes away from him as he drives through the crowded streets of New York.

Christmas lights twinkle along the streets, and snow lightly falls, but I can't take my eyes off Edison. The muscles in his arms flex as he steers, his hand gripping the wheel with that one-handed spin—the one that makes all girls want to lose their panties, lie back, and demand those hands be touching their bodies.

He's bringing out my inner slut, and while it scares the hell out of me, my mind is starting to align with the traitor between my thighs.

"Stop looking at me like that, Sydney."

"How am I looking at you?"

"Like you want my fingers back in your tight little cunt."

I remain silent, biting on my lip and trying my damn hardest to calm my racing and smutty thoughts, thinking about all the times I've read about a woman sucking off a guy while he's driving. Realistically, it's probably not the safest idea—but if I don't get out of this car soon, I might just say screw it and beg him to pull over.

Chapter 10

Sydney

A few minutes later, we pull up in front of a cozy little bar tucked away in the snow-dusted streets. Edison slips his warm hand in mine, sending a rush of butterflies through my stomach as we make our way inside.

Fucking butterflies—one day, I might have to thank him for reminding me what they feel like, but right now, I would like them to control themselves.

Twinkling string lights and flickering candles inside the bar give it a festive vibe while all I can smell is pine and cinnamon, making me feel like I've just been snowglobed straight into a Hallmark holiday movie.

Once we reach the bar, Edison orders a whiskey for himself and a glass of wine for me. He leans against the counter with me by his side, and his hand finds its place at the small of my back, his thumb tracing slow, lazy circles on my skin. I practically melt into him, my body leaning closer as if it's got a mind of its own, and when I look up at him, I find him already watching me, like he knows exactly how my body reacts to his touch.

With our drinks in hand, Edison guides me to a quiet corner table tucked away by the window, where the soft glow from the Christmas lights filters through the frosted glass. Like a gentleman, he pulls out my chair, gesturing for me to sit while he takes the seat across from me. He leans back, tilting his head slightly, and his eyes don't just meet mine—they hold me there, pinning me in place.

"So, you want to explain what that shit was all about tonight? Because I gotta tell you, Sydney, I'm not here to fuck around. Games aren't my thing, and I won't play them. It doesn't matter how into you I am."

Yeah, he just got even hotter.

"They're not mine either, but given what happened last night with you and that other woman, I wouldn't normally agree to another date. I'm not the kind of girl who tolerates being messed around. I've been there, done that, and I have the ex to prove it."

"I explained what happened."

"No, you didn't, and it's fine because it's your business." He leans in closer, propping his elbows on the table and clasping his hands together in front of his mouth.

"You think I'm lying."

"I don't," I say, shaking my head as I lift my glass, "but you're holding back the truth."

"When it comes to my clients' privacy and safety, I have to be extremely careful about the information I share."

"And I get that, but when someone asks where you keep your wine because you're going to a hotel..." I trail off as my eyes catch his. "It screams, 'I'm planning on spending the night inside someone else.'"

Edison lets out a sigh, dragging his hand over his jaw as if trying to rub away the tension. "I can see how it might've looked that way, but that's not what was happening."

"But you can understand why it makes me think twice about what I'm possibly getting into, right?"

"And what is it you think you're getting into?"

"You tell me," I counter, shrugging as I keep my eyes on his.

"I can give you some explanation, but not all of it, Sydney," he says. "I understand why you reacted the way you did, and I want to offer you something here so you stop thinking I'm a prick." With a heavy sigh, he leans back in his chair, tracing his finger along the rim of his glass before finally speaking. "The woman you heard in my house was my ex-girlfriend," he confesses, tilting his head to the side as he tries to gauge my reaction.

Awesome. It's even worse than I thought.

"I think I preferred not knowing."

"Whatever was between us is long dead, I assure you. I can't stand the woman, which is why, when I found out she was coming to me as a client, I made sure my team was at my house so that we wouldn't be alone." He speaks calmly, but I notice the slight tension in his body as he runs a hand through his dark hair. "Going to a hotel with her was never part of the plan. We were trying to find her a place to stay."

"It's fine, Edison. We're not in a relationship. We're just—" I fall silent as he cuts me off.

"Getting to know each other but also desperate to find out how it's going to feel when we do actually fuck."

He's so naked in my head right now.

"Yeah, something like that," I murmur, feeling fucking feral.

"So, I have a question for you." He settles back into his chair, stretching his arms out and casually resting his glass on the armrest.

"I've been upfront with you about wanting to get to know you, but am I wasting my time here?"

His openness and utter lack of fear in communicating everything he's feeling only add to the pull I feel toward him.

"No matter how you answer that question, I'll still take you home tonight and fuck you to within an inch of your life if that's what you want, but I need to know if that's all you're looking for from me."

My mind races, caught between the lure of his promise and the fear that letting him in could mean losing myself in a way I've never allowed before.

"No, that's not all I want, but I'm hard work, Edison."

"I'm not afraid to put in the work when the connection is this strong."

"I don't allow anyone in, and I'm especially closed off to men."

"Then maybe I can change that."

"I'll repeatedly push you away."

"Then I'll push back until you get tired of it."

He snaps back at everything I throw at him, but I can't stop myself from wondering what it'll take for him to turn and run. Maybe I'm testing his limits to save him from me, or maybe it's because my heart won't survive another blow, and Edison is the type of guy a girl could definitely lose her heart to.

"I hate cooking."

"I'll cook, or you can let me take you to dinner."

I pause before speaking to catch my breath, fully aware that my next words have the potential to be a deal-breaker.

"I would only quit my job if it was something I wanted to do. Not because someone asked me to."

"You think I wanna change you? I don't, baby, not at all. I know what you have to do to provide for yourself, and I'm still borderline stalking your ass just to get you to spend a little time with me. I'm a secure man, Sydney—jealous at times, admittedly, maybe possessive to a point, but only because I know what I want and will do whatever I can to keep it. But controlling? No, never."

"I don't understand what this is, so why are you pushing so hard for me?"

"Because you feel like fire, baby, and I've lived in the cold for far too long."

Merry Christmas, Sydney. You've just found yourself a husband.

I shake my head, blonde strands falling around my face as I try to clear my thoughts. "You could have anyone you want, Edison, and you know it," I say, gazing up at him and tucking my hair behind my ears.

"You want the truth?" he asks, and I nod, unable to tear my eyes away from him. "I've dated many women in the past, and I've messed around a lot. But that's not who I am now. I want one woman—a woman who I connect with on a level that exceeds anything I have ever felt—someone who gets me, who challenges me, and who makes me want to be better. I want a woman I can build a life with. Someone I'll still be completely obsessed with when we're both old and gray."

I tilt my head and raise an eyebrow at him. "Speaking of old and gray," I tease, as a playful smile tugs at the corners of my lips.

He throws his head back and releases a deep, hearty laugh, causing the faintest of lines to form at the corners of his silver eyes. "Hey, I'm not old or gray yet, beautiful."

Throw me down and call me beautiful while you take control of me.

"Do you always go for younger women?" I ask, fully aware that he'll already know I'm twenty-nine since he did some digging on me.

"Not intentionally. Besides, I'm only ten years older than you, which is nothing," he shrugs.

"Hey, it works for me. I'm into older guys."

His lips curl into a devastating smile, one I'm dying to kiss off his perfect face. "I guess that's one good thing we've got going for us then."

"I think we've got more than just that going for us, Edison." His teeth graze against his bottom lip, and he nods, silently acknowledging the undeniable chemistry that's crackling between us. "So you're rich, huh?" I tease, and his laughter fills the space between us again.

"And yet, my money doesn't impress you." His eyes meet mine as his hand gently glides across the rough stubble on his jaw. "Are you sure you're real?"

"Don't get me wrong, I love having money; that's why I do what I do. But I see people at their worst when they believe they're entitled to whatever they want as long as they can afford it."

"That was how you felt about me the first night I came to see you at the club, wasn't it?"

I nod, my mind going back to that night. "I was so mad at you for that because I wanted you to be different from them."

"I'm sorry if it seemed that way, but I promise you I'm not like them," he says, his eyes softening as he understands exactly what I'm referring to—the Huxley Fosters of the world. "You've just been driving me fucking crazy since the moment I laid eyes on you."

"I was too quick to judge you without giving you a fair chance," I admit, and he offers me the warmest smile. "I have a question for you now."

"Go for it, baby. I'm an open book."

"Do you date more than one woman at a time? Because I won't date someone who's seeing multiple women. So if I'm just one of many, I'd rather know now."

"I only date with the possibility of a future," he firmly states, his eyes burning into mine. "I refuse to waste anyone's time or lead them on, and if I can't see myself building a life with them, then it's not worth pursuing."

He reaches across the table, and just like that, my heart stumbles. His hand finds mine, his fingers sliding between each space, lacing together as if they've done this a thousand times before.

"What about you? Are you seeing other people?" he asks, his voice dripping with possessiveness. "By the way, your answer had better be no, or I'll be demanding a name."

"It's hard enough letting one guy in, let alone any more than that, so no, it's only you."

"You've been hurt," he says gently after a moment of silence.

It's not a question—he can see it, feel it.

"Yeah, it was pretty brutal, and it's something I never want to go through again."

"Can I ask what happened?"

I love the way he looks at me, the way it makes me feel. I never know if his eyes are saying, "Trust me, I'm here for you. Show me what the world doesn't see—the parts you keep hidden" or "I'm here for you, and I'm going to fuck you till you forget your name." But honestly, I find myself wanting both sides of him.

"A friend of mine who I met while working at the club—well, ex-friend now—came to live with me and my boyfriend because she was fairly new to the city, and we had a spare room." His long, dark lashes flicker shut for a split second, knowing exactly how this story is about to unfold. His grip on my hand tightens, silently offering me comfort. "One night, I got off work early and found my boyfriend on the kitchen floor with his ass in the air, fucking her." A shudder ripples through me as I remember Charlie's moans of pleasure directed toward someone who wasn't me, and for a moment, I get lost in the memory of that beautifully wrapped box of shit I call my ex. I've tried to bury the image deep in my mind, but how do you ever really get over seeing the person you love balls deep in somebody else?

"I went and stayed with my mom, but when I eventually met with him to have a conversation a week later, he told me that she was pregnant. He said they would be living at our apartment together and asked me to move my shit out."

The expression on Edison's face sets me on edge but in the best way. "Give me a name. I know plenty of people in this city who would be more than happy to tear up a piece of shit like that."

I wave him off, not knowing if he's joking, but I'm almost positive he isn't. "It doesn't matter anymore. It happened, and yes, it left me with some trust issues, but who doesn't have parts of them that aren't a little screwed up? Besides, karma fucked him in the ass. Cora found out a while back that the kid wasn't even his."

"I'm sorry you had to go through that, baby. Some people really should've been swallowed." A fit of unladylike laughter escapes me before I can stop it, and Edison's smile stretches wider, his perfect teeth on display. "Whatever happens between us here happens. But I need you to know that I would never do anything to hurt you. Listen..." he continues, his voice dropping to a husky whisper. "We might wake up tomorrow feeling nothing, but I don't ever remember feeling this way about someone I just met—that urge to get to know them, that sexual chemistry that you can't force, and I would really like to explore it with you."

Chapter 11
Edison

A couple of hours have passed since we started talking, and I can't shake this unfamiliar feeling in my chest. It's a feeling I've been searching for—one I'd almost given up on ever finding—yet here I am, sitting across from this goddess, and it's burning inside me like wildfire.

Being around Sydney always has me on the brink of either calmness or chaos. I've never met anyone who can drive me to the edge of insanity and yet also make me feel completely at ease.

She's strong, but her heart is bruised.

She just needs someone to treat her a little differently, love her a little harder, and reassure her a little more.

"Are you close with your mom?" I ask, knowing that's who she turned to when her prick of an ex stupidly threw her away—yet I'm grateful because it means I get to sit here with her now.

"We are. It's not like I call her every day or tell her about every little problem I might have, but we go for brunch sometimes. Once a month, I go over for Mexican food. We have little traditions like that."

"That must be nice."

"Yeah, it is. My dad left when I was a baby—pulled the whole 'I'm just going out for milk' act and never came back. It was just me and my mom for a while."

"Jesus, it's no wonder you hate men." I can't help but laugh, but it pains me knowing that she's been so let down her entire life.

"Not true. I just hate certain types of men, and I have a low tolerance for bullshit. My mom met a good one when I was nine, Geoff, and he's been like a father to me over the past twenty years."

I'm glad not every man in her life has broken her, and I'm determined to be the one who proves we're not all pieces of shit. She deserves someone who won't tear her down, who'll be there in the shadows, unshakable, even when she's ready to run.

"What about you? Are you close to your parents?" Sydney's pretty green eyes meet mine as she asks, but I hesitate, glancing down at the table and taking a deep breath before answering.

"They actually passed away a long time ago now."

Her eyes widen, and she brings her hand to her mouth in shock. "Oh my god, Edison, I'm so sorry."

"Don't worry. It's a normal question for anyone to ask," I say calmly, giving her a reassuring smile and hoping to ease her because I can see she thinks she just shoved her foot down her throat. "I was twenty-three when I lost my mom. She'd been sick since I was young, so we were all prepared."

"I can't imagine that makes it any easier."

"It doesn't, but at least we were able to say goodbye." I pause before taking a sip of my drink—water now as I have to drive this beautiful woman home safely tonight. "Then my dad left us peacefully in his sleep a few weeks later. It was like he'd given up and couldn't live without her, and his soul had to go find her."

The memories flood back, bittersweet and painful all at once. But there's comfort in knowing they loved each other so much that even death couldn't keep them apart.

"I'm sorry you lost him too, but imagine having a love like that."

"Why do you think I am the way that I am?" Her smile is not one of sympathy but of understanding. "I'm the product of two people who were lucky enough to find their soulmate."

"No wonder you move so damn fast," she murmurs, her lips twisting into a hunger-filled smile that mirrors the sexual tension that's been simmering between us all night.

"Do you want another drink?"

Say no, and let me get you the hell out of here.

Sydney shakes her head, and before I can even think, I'm on my feet, holding my hand out toward her. She takes it, standing slowly, and the warmth of her palm steadies me. I tighten my hold, just enough to make it clear that I'm not letting her go.

Not here, not tonight.

Together, we head toward the door, weaving through the crowded bar. I keep her close—so close that I feel the soft brush of her shoulder against mine with every step.

As soon as we reach my car, I press her back against the door with a force that pulls a gasp from her lips. All around us, light snow drifts down, each flake vanishing the instant it touches her flushed skin. My hands find her hips, gripping firmly as I pull her closer, erasing any hint of space between us, as though fusing our bodies together is the only thing that will satisfy this ache.

"I can't kiss you here, baby, because if I kiss you, I won't be able to stop. And if I don't stop, I'll bend you over right here and fuck you until you can't think straight."

Her fingers tangle in my shirt, pulling me closer, like she's daring me to lose control. "You already know I like to be watched," she replies, her voice dripping with sex.

"Get in the car, Sydney," I command, reaching behind her and pulling open the door. She slips into the passenger seat, and I close the door with a click. Rounding the front of the car, my pulse pounds in my ears, and I settle into the driver's seat.

"How long?" she asks, and I turn my head to meet her gaze.

"Too fucking long," I grit out, barely getting the words out before she reaches for me, pulling me in until our lips collide.

When I groan, she whimpers into my mouth, the sound only throwing more fuel on the fire raging between us. Her fingers thread through my hair, tugging me closer as I deepen the kiss, pouring everything I have into it because I don't think I've ever been kissed like this—like she needs me in this all-consuming way. Every touch, every press of her lips, and every lick of her mouth feeds a craving inside me—a growing addiction to the way this woman makes me feel.

Maybe it's her no-fucks-given personality or the way she unapologetically calls me out and puts me in my place, but when it comes to touching her, when it comes to intimacy, I want to own every damn part of her. The contrast between her stubbornness and the way she surrenders herself to my touch only deepens my need to claim her.

"I'm going to drive, and you're going to touch yourself." I say as I start the car and pull out onto the road. "Show me what I've been craving since I had my fingers inside your pussy." I glance between her and the road, my pulse quickening as she slowly lifts her dress, revealing smooth, golden skin and lace-covered curves. My throat tightens as I watch her fingers hover by the sides of her panties. "Leave them on, baby. Slip them to the side and spread yourself open for me."

My focus on the road becomes almost non-existent. She pulls the lace aside, and my mouth goes dry. Her fingers move over her clit, but it's the look on her face that nearly undoes me—the way her head rolls back, eyes heavy-lidded as she gets lost in the pleasure she's creating.

"So fucking beautiful," I growl, the memory slamming into me of how goddamn hard I was with my fingers buried deep inside her, feeling every tight pulse of her body.

And now here I am, aching for her all over again.

I want to be the one who knows exactly how to satisfy her, the one she trusts to be there, ready to indulge in every filthy little fantasy she has.

She likes to be watched—she told me as much—and I can see she's getting off on exposing herself like this in front of me. There's something so raw and vulnerable about it, and knowing she's giving me this part of herself stirs emotions I shouldn't be feeling, especially since I'm still getting to know her.

She slides a finger inside herself, gasping in a way that makes jealousy flare inside me because I want it to be me pulling those sounds out of her.

"I'm so wet for you, Edison." Her voice is a teasing whisper that barely reaches my ears, yet I catch every fucking word.

The slick, shameless sound of her fingers plunging inside herself is unmistakable, and her soft whimpers drive me out of my mind.

The second she withdraws her finger, I reach across and capture her wrist. My eyes stay fixed on the road as I suck her finger into my mouth, ready to drown myself in her.

"Fuck, I can't. You gotta stop," I snap, lowering the window to try and cool the fire raging inside me. "Keep your hands where I can see them."

A cocky smirk forms on her lips as she sits up in her seat. "What's the matter, handsome? You wish it were your fingers inside me."

"Something like that," I reply, my grip tightening on the wheel until my knuckles turn white. My vision blurs, and my entire body vibrates with the need to touch her, wreck her, and make her scream my name until it's the only word she knows. It takes everything in me not to slam on the brakes, pull over to the side of the road, and tear those flimsy panties off her. I want to bury my face between her thighs and taste her until she's shaking, until she's lost in me and what I can do to her body. The thought alone almost sends me over the edge. "You're mine tonight, baby. To touch, taste, and fucking own. Every scream from your lips will belong to me."

Chapter 12

Edison

The rest of the drive is a tense, silent battle of self-control. When I finally pull up to my house, I ignore her eyes widening at its size, too focused on getting her inside. I get out and open the door for her, and without a word, I take her hand and lead her through the fresh snow that crunches beneath our feet.

I slam the front door shut behind me, the sound echoing in the heavy silence between us. With a curl of my finger, I beckon her to come closer, and she doesn't hesitate, pushing me back against the door with a force that rattles the frame.

Her lips move against mine, hungry and demanding, like she's hellbent on devouring me whole, and all I can focus on is the moment I'll have my mouth between her legs, kissing her pussy just as deeply.

I'm lost in her.

Being wanted like this—needed so desperately—is fucking addictive.

Her hands fall to my hips, and she begins to tear at my clothes, unfastening my pants. As I rake my hands through my hair, my zipper comes down.

She steps back, kicking off her heels, and my hands itch to reach inside my pants and grip my cock.

"Bring that mouth back over here." She steps back into my space and rises on her toes, her tongue tracing a slow, teasing line up my neck.

My hands drop to her waist, gripping tight as she continues her torturously slow ascent, her tongue tracing every ridge and leaving a trail of heat in its wake. When her tongue finally reaches my jaw and moves toward my mouth, I lower my lips to hers, and she moans—fucking moans—and my dick is practically begging to be freed.

She slips a hand inside my pants, wrapping her fingers around my cock. My head falls back against the door with a thud, and a ragged breath claws its way from my chest as her touch unravels me with every stroke.

"You really do live up to that big dick energy, don't you?"

"Let's see if you're still this excited when it hits the back of your throat and you lose the ability to breathe."

Her emerald eyes lock onto mine, and she sinks to her knees before me, challenging me. She glides her hands up my thighs before she tugs down my jeans and boxer briefs and releases me. I'm mesmerized as I watch her lean in, and with a slow, deliberate lick, her tongue collects the bead of precum that's gathered at the tip.

"You're all wound up, Edison."

My breath hisses out between clenched teeth as she wraps her warm, wet mouth around the head of my cock.

"Stop being a tease," I rasp, the roughness in my voice showing just how goddamn needy I am for her.

That smirk on her beautiful mouth has me aching to ruin her.

Her hand wraps firmly around my cock, squeezing from base to tip, her eyes dark with intent as she licks her lips. Without wasting another second, she sinks her mouth over me, inch by inch, moving slow and sensual, like she's savoring this for her own satisfaction—every shudder, every twitch, all of it driving her need.

"Fuuuck," the word tears out of me in a guttural moan as I inhale sharply, her throat taking me all the way down while my hands tangle in her platinum strands that glide through my fingers like silk. "That's it, baby, just like that," I groan, watching her full pink lips stretch around me, driving me fucking wild, and when she looks up at me through her lashes, it only makes me harder.

She's got me right where she wants me, owning the fuck out of me, and I'm more than ready to hand over whatever she asks for.

God, she could suck a man's soul out of him.

Fuck it, I'll give it to her willingly at this point.

I thrust deeper—deep enough that I hear her gag—and the sound is pure sin. "As badly as I want to come down your throat, I need to feel that pussy around me."

But she doesn't listen. Instead, she sucks hard, cheeks hollowing out as she works my cock in a way that nearly drives me over the edge.

"God, you're perfect," I whisper, fixated on her face.

She draws back and releases me, looking up at me through eyes that are now glistening with tears.

Fucking beautiful.

"You're not getting my pussy unless you give me what I want." Her voice is laced with a thirst I'm more than willing to quench.

"And what is it you want, beautiful?"

"I want your cum, Edison." As she fists my cock with one hand, she flattens her tongue and runs it over my balls. "I want you to fuck my mouth and watch as I swallow every last drop of you."

Yeah, she's got wife written all over her.

I give her a nod—my silent permission for her to take whatever she wants from me. Her hands slide up the front of my T-shirt, and her nails scratch lightly across my abs as she arches her back, positioning herself perfectly and offering her mouth up for me to use.

My hands return to her hair, and I begin to thrust, each move of my hips driven by this raw primal need. When her throat opens, I push deeper, and I feel her take me fully. It's like nothing I've ever experienced—the heat, the way she gags slightly but doesn't pull back, and the way she stays exactly where she is while I fuck her throat.

Her nails bite into my skin as her eyes flutter shut, and I watch a tear slip down her cheek, but her lips stretch into a smile around me as if this is exactly what she wants. She's right here with me, matching my hunger, and I know I've met my match in her.

"Feels so fucking good, baby." I groan as my breath comes in quick, labored, bursts and my hips thrust faster. "You suck my dick like you were made for it."

Pressure coils tightly in my stomach, and a wave of heat spreads up my spine. I didn't realize how badly I needed her to take the edge off until now.

"Fuck, yes, I'm coming."

She hums softly, gripping the base of my cock, and a strangled groan rips from my chest as I start to come.

"Don't swallow it. You fucking hold it, Sydney." I slow my thrusts, allowing her to control the pace as I continue to spill inside her mouth. Once I pull out, I gently lift her chin with my hand. "Open up, baby. Show me." She does as I say, parting her lips and showing me her mouth full of my cum. "That's my girl. Now swallow."

Her throat bobs, and I notice a trace of me left on her lower lip. Reaching down, I scoop it up with my thumb and slide it into her mouth.

I pull her to her feet and lift her into my arms, her legs wrapping tightly around my waist, holding on like she has no intention of letting go.

My semi-hard cock brushes against the delicate lace of her underwear, teasing both of us with just enough friction that I'm half a second away from ripping them off and taking her right here against the wall. Instead, I capture her mouth, pressing my lips to hers with a hunger that edges on desperation as I carry her up the stairs to my room, savoring the faint taste of myself that lingers on her tongue.

She lifts her dress over her head, tossing it aside so it lands in a crumpled heap on the wooden steps. Heart pounding, I kick the bedroom door open and stride toward the bed, laying her down. My fingers find the edges of her thong, tugging it away as she reaches behind to unhook her bra, letting it slip from her shoulders and drop to the floor.

Sydney's lying completely naked before me, every inch of her body exposed, ready, and so fucking tempting that it feels almost criminal.

"Jesus, you're beautiful, baby," I whisper, my voice filled with awe as I start to peel off my clothes.

I climb onto the bed and hover over her, our bodies so close but barely touching. Leaning in slowly, I press my lips to hers, feeling her melt into the kiss as her body arches up to meet mine.

There's no rush to this kiss, none of that usual, desperate pull that's almost taken us over every other time. Right now, I just want to savor her—the slow, soft press of her lips, the subtle sweetness of her taste, the silky slide of her tongue moving with mine. She's here, finally beneath me, and I'm taking my time, letting each second sink in, memorizing every touch, every breath.

Even though I've only just come, my body is already burning for her again. I trail kisses down her neck, along her collarbone, until I reach her beautiful breasts.

My lips latch onto her nipple, sucking it until it hardens against my tongue while my hand glides slowly down her body. She trembles beneath my touch, and when I finally reach between her legs, I take my time, teasing her with the lightest graze of my fingertips. I slowly work my mouth over her nipple, building her up until I can't hold back any longer.

I plunge a finger deep inside her, then add another, feeling her walls grip me as my thumb grazes her swollen clit.

"Was it sucking my cock that made you this wet, baby?"

"Yes," she cries out before I slam my lips against hers in a bruising kiss, stealing her breath and her moans, swallowing them whole as my fingers press against that soft spot inside her.

Pulling my fingers away, I move down her body, tracing my tongue along her silky skin until my face nestles between her legs. Her eyes, dark and glazed over with need, lock onto mine as I look up at her.

"I haven't stopped thinking about eating this pussy."

"Then put your mouth on me already, Edison," she pleads.

Her fingers tangle in my hair, tugging hard as she guides me closer. I press my nose against her and breathe her in, letting her scent leave its mark on me. It's intoxicating. I lift my eyes to hers again, needing to see her face as I take that first long lick of her cunt. Flattening my tongue, I drag it over her, savoring the way she shudders beneath me and the way her eyes roll back when I do it again.

I pull her clit into my mouth, sucking gently while my tongue flutters against her. But I want more than just this moment—I want complete control over her.

I slide my hands up her legs and pin her down against the bed, holding her thighs wide apart, keeping her right where I want her.

"You taste so fucking good." She tries to buck her hips, to grind herself against my face, but I hold her steady and draw out every second of having her laid bare before me.

I spread her thighs wider, pushing them further up the bed, wanting every inch of her exposed to me.

"Please, don't stop," she begs, her voice a shaky whisper.

"Stay with me, baby. I'm not done with you yet." My tongue is lapping and sucking with a desperation that's been building up inside me since the moment I first heard her voice.

She's made me work for this—harder than I've ever had to before—but now, with her sprawled out before me, every second of that delicious torture feels worth it.

Sydney writhes beneath me, her body straining against my hold, and I hope like hell I'm leaving marks on her skin so that she remembers this moment every time she looks at them.

Her arousal coats my lips, and I'm pretty sure I'm hooked. Her taste, her scent—it's everywhere, wrapping around me, sinking under my skin.

"Fuck, fuck, fuck, yes, right there," she cries out, her voice trembling as her orgasm begins to crest.

Her hands fist in my hair, and I welcome the sting as I feel her body coil beneath me, every muscle tensing as she reaches the edge. Her body erupts within seconds, and she screams for me as her climax crashes through her.

"Holy shit," she pants, her breath ragged as I suck her orgasm from her.

I crawl back up her body, capturing her lips so she can taste herself and know just how hard she came for me.

"I'm going to fuck you so deep that when you wake up, you'll still feel me between your legs." My cock brushes against her slick cunt, desperate to find its way inside her.

She lifts her head from the pillow, her lips brushing against mine. "Then I suggest you hurry up and get that big dick inside me."

"Get on your knees," I command, watching as she positions herself in front of me and bends over, giving me the perfect view of her ass.

I reach for a condom because we stupidly forgot to have that conversation, and I hate myself for it, especially when all I want is to fuck her bare and fill her with my cum.

Screw it, she looks like she'd nail being a mom.

I shut down the intrusive thoughts and refocus on the woman spread out in front of me—because priorities.

I pull her back against my chest, lifting her until she's flush against me. My hands roam over her skin, fingers grazing down her curves until they find her hardened nipples.

"You're so perfect," I murmur, trailing soft kisses along her shoulder, feeling the warmth of her body respond as goosebumps rise under my touch. "So perfect for me, Sydney." I bring one hand to her throat, cupping it as I turn her face toward mine. "Where have you been?" I ask, lowering my forehead to hers.

"Waiting for you to find me," she whispers, her voice so soft it barely reaches my ears.

The moment my eyes lock on her green orbs, it's as if the world stops. My chest tightens, and the steady rhythm of my heartbeat shifts, slamming against my ribcage.

I press my mouth to hers, and what starts slow and passionate quickly turns into something desperate and demanding.

"Bend that ass over and show me how well you can take me." She leans forward on the bed, and my inked hands grip her hips, my stark black tattoos contrasting beautifully against her golden skin.

I spread her open, running my tongue from her clit to her ass, and the taste of her drives me wild.

I line myself up with her, the head of my cock pressing against her entrance. I start to push inside, and a rush of pleasure slams into me, taking my breath away.

"Fuck, Edison!"

"You can take me, baby. Just breathe and let me in."

My eyes are focused on the sight of my cock slowly disappearing inside her, and I'm getting off purely on the way she stretches to take me in.

"That's it, just a little bit more." Her moans make it impossible to hold back, making me want to completely lose myself in her. "Fuck, I wish you could see this, the way you're welcoming me inside you."

I need more.

More of her, more of this connection—*just more.*

I pull out of her and quickly flip her onto her back—I need to see her face as I drive myself inside her again. I hook her leg around my waist and thrust in deep, fucking her savagely as my hips pound between her thighs.

I can't get close enough; every move I make is fueled by the need to feel her, to lose myself in this.

There's no hiding, no pretending. This is real, and it's taking over every part of me—my body, my thoughts, my heart. Right now, it's all hers.

My hand slides down between us, fingers finding her clit, while my other hand weaves through hers before pinning it above her head.

"You look so fucking pretty with my cock inside you." I grind into her, pushing even deeper. "Now give it up to me, Sydney," I growl, my need to possess her taking over completely.

Our eyes connect, and when her cunt clenches around me, she screams out. The delicious sting of her nails dragging down my back brings me closer to climax. I'm right there with her, and with one, two, three final thrusts, my orgasm tears through my body.

Our bodies are slick with sweat, and her delicate fingers trace lazy, tender strokes along my back as we come down from the high we just shared.

Dipping my head, I place a lingering kiss against her lips before slowly pulling out and rolling to the side. I discard the condom, slip back under the covers, and slide in beside her, tucking my body next to hers. My fingers drift to her thigh, tracing patterns over her skin, like I'm trying to hold onto every second. This need to stay connected, to keep touching her, feels instinctual—something I can't ignore.

"I hate to feed your ego, but that was pretty amazing."

"I don't think there are words to describe how incredible that was," I add, but I can still feel her reluctance to let me in.

Physically, she's allowed us to get as close as two people can, but emotionally, it's a different story. Breaking through those walls and getting into her mind will take time and effort—something I'm more than willing to do because whatever has happened to me since we met makes me believe that this could really be something.

"So what happens now? I didn't exactly bring an overnight bag," she says, turning that playful smile toward me.

I turn to face her and gently cup her cheek. "Well, I'm going to take you into the shower and eat your pussy again, because, fuck, baby, you taste so damn good, and I haven't had nearly enough." My thumb brushes along her lips, tugging on the lower one, remembering how they felt wrapped around my dick earlier tonight. "Then I'm going to pin you against the tiles and fuck you until you come on my cock again."

"Is that your way of asking if I'd like to stay the night?" Her smile widens, but I can hear it—the uncertainty in her words, like she's unsure if I want her to stay or if I'm considering taking her home.

"I'm not asking, Sydney," I say, tucking a stray piece of platinum hair behind her ear. "Besides, I knew you'd be spending the night in my bed when I found you at the club."

That feeling I've been chasing—this is it.

Chapter 13

Sydney

Edison didn't let me get much sleep last night, but I'm not complaining. He pushed my body to the brink, and after orgasm number six, he decided to just hold me for the rest of the night instead. I know because I woke up wrapped in his arms, his body curled protectively around mine. Even in sleep, his grip was territorial, making sure I knew that, at least for the night, I was entirely his.

Last night was nothing short of phenomenal. The chemistry between us was undeniable, but it was his ability to get inside my head and connect with me on a level that went beyond physical. He didn't just make my body surrender. He owned every thought and every breath until all that was left was him.

This thing between us is still so new, but it's intense, and I'm not sure how to handle how he makes me feel when I've spent so long building a concrete wall around my heart. I want to let him in, but there's this nagging voice in the back of my mind telling me that he might wake up today and be over this fascination he's had with me. Now that I've given in to him, I can't help but wonder if maybe one night with me was enough.

I feel Edison stir behind me, his body slowly waking up as his arm tightens around my waist. His warm breath tickles the back of my neck while his morning wood presses firmly into my back.

No wonder he's so confident, given what he's working with.

A quiet chuckle escapes me because I honestly have no idea where this guy gets his energy from. After everything we did last night, he should be exhausted.

"Good morning, baby."

"How did you know I was awake?"

"You finally stopped snoring," he teases, and I spin around in his arms, ready to fire back at him. However, as soon as I see him, my words fade away. His eyes are still closed, and I get lost in the sleepy smile tugging at his lips. His hair is ruffled messily across his forehead, and something about seeing him like this—so carefree and relaxed—sets the butterflies in my stomach fluttering.

"I do not snore," I protest, and he laughs, the deep rumble of his morning voice sounding even sexier than usual.

"No, you don't. But you do breathe a little differently."

"I guess that's just one more thing you've noticed about me."

"That, and after last night, I've definitely learned a few more things."

"Yeah? Like what?"

"Like how you moan every time I kiss you," he murmurs, his voice low as he leans in and ghosts his lips over my jaw. "Does my tongue do something to you, baby?"

His lips trail along my neck, lingering just enough that my body responds instantly, and heat pools low in my belly.

"In the last twelve hours, your tongue has done a lot to me," I rasp, my voice thick with desire as his hand slides into my hair, gripping tightly at the nape of my neck. He wraps it in his fist, tilting my head back and exposing my throat to him. I can feel the control he has over me as he drags his tongue slowly along my neck, leaving a trail of heat before it finds its way back into my mouth. "You're making it impossible to even think about leaving this bed."

"Then stay here and let me indulge in your body."

He hooks my leg around his waist, pulling me tight against him as his hips lift, letting me feel just how hard he is as he presses against my core. Each slow, deliberate grind against my clit sends a spark through me, rekindling the sensations from last night and reigniting every touch and every moment we shared.

His tongue possesses my mouth, and he caresses me between my thighs before he slides a finger inside me. "Let's get this pussy nice and wet," he whispers against my lips. He pumps me, slow and deep, each thrust making me tremble before he pulls out, spreading my arousal as his fingers trail over my ass. My breath hitches, and a sharp gasp escapes me as his thumb brushes over my untouched hole.

"Holy shit." My eyes snap open, and I watch as lust drives his every move.

"Have you ever been touched here?" he asks, and I shake my head while he continues to circle his thumb.

I think I like it. No, I definitely like it.

"You want me to fill your ass, Sydney? Because I wanna fuck every part of you." All I can do is nod, my body already halfway to losing control. "That's my girl," he whispers, "but right now, I'm gonna fuck this pussy until you're screaming my name and I'm drenched in your cum."

His dirty mouth is going to be the end of me.

He lowers his head and roughly sucks my nipple into his mouth, growling as he struggles to contain his hunger for me.

"Turn around," he demands, and I twist in his arms, pushing my ass back into him. "Patience, greedy girl."

"I need you inside me already." His chuckle fills my ears, and I hear a wrapper being torn.

"I can't wait for the day I get to fill this perfect pussy."

"I'm covered."

He buries his face into my hair, breathing in deeply before letting out a low moan. "You can't just say that to a man."

"I want to feel you, Edison."

"For someone who held out on me for so long, you sure are needy now."

"That's because you give great dick. Now shut up and fuck me." He wraps his fingers around my throat and presses his solid body against my back, his teeth brushing against the shell of my ear.

"If you want to come, beautiful, then I suggest you watch your fucking mouth," he growls as he fills me inch by thick inch, and the sheer size of him steals my breath.

"Edison..."

"Shh... you can take it," he murmurs, his voice low and steady, soothing as he pulls me closer, grounding us both in the moment. "So tight. So perfect."

His hot breath brushes my shoulder as the hand decorating my throat tightens slightly. I meet him thrust for thrust, backing into him and taking every inch of his cock with each powerful drive of his hips while his free hand explores my body.

He leans in close and whispers into my ear, "Touch yourself for me."

My hand lowers between my legs, and my fingers glide over my clit. The sounds that escape my lips are those of a lust-crazed woman who's never truly been fucked properly—at least not like this.

"Do you know what your pussy feels like to me, Sydney?"

"Tell me," I rasp out, barely able to form the words.

"It feels like it was made for me and my cock."

His teeth sink into my shoulder with a sharp bite of pleasure before he soothes the skin with his tongue.

"Now fucking come for me," he demands, his voice thick with need. "Tighten that cunt around me, Sydney. Let me feel it." His words tip me headfirst over the edge, and I clench around him as I detonate, screaming his name as my orgasm crashes through me. "Fuck, that's it. That's my girl."

For a moment, he slows, letting me ride out the waves of my climax and catch my breath, but then he picks up speed again, slamming into me relentlessly.

"Use me, baby. Fill me with your cum." I gasp with each thrust, my body still trembling and oversensitive from the aftershocks of my orgasm.

"Give me your tongue."

I turn my face to his, and the moment our lips meet, the power of his kiss obliterates any memory of those who came before him. His fucking becomes wilder and more uncontrolled as he feeds savagely on my mouth.

His steel eyes meet mine, and I whisper against his lips, "Come for me." With one final, powerful thrust, he unleashes a roar, and his entire body shudders as his release crashes through him.

He sighs and buries his face in the curve of my neck, wrapping his arms around me like he never wants to let me go.

"Fuck, baby."

The scent of us—sweat, sex, and something uniquely ours—fills the air, and I find myself completely lost in a state of pure bliss and utter fucking contentment.

"Stay with me today," he murmurs, placing a soft kiss on my bare shoulder. "I'm not ready to let you go yet."

"I would but I have to work."

"At Cora's?" he asks, and I turn in his arms. My breasts brush against his chest, and I let my fingers glide up to the back of his neck before I weave them through his hair.

I nod, pressing a kiss against his jaw. "I'm not back at the club until tomorrow."

"So you're free tonight?"

"No, sorry, I'm crazy busy tonight."

"That right?" he asks as his lips curl into a smirk.

"Yeah, you see, I plan to be fucked all over my apartment by this insanely handsome guy who's got my head in a spin," I reply, watching his smirk deepen.

"He sounds like a lucky guy."

"He is, but he knows I can't really cook, so I hope he's down for Thai."

His hands trail up my spine, pulling me closer to him until our bodies press together. "I'm pretty sure he loves Thai."

Of all the ways Edison has touched me, this moment feels the most intimate. His hands aren't just on my skin; they're reaching deeper, unraveling something locked away inside me. I can feel myself opening up to him in ways I never thought possible—letting my walls crumble, piece by piece.

As our foreheads press together and I sink deeper into this connection, a loud banging echoes from his front door, shattering this bubble we've created.

"Do you usually get visitors this early?"

"I don't usually get visitors unless they're scheduled months in advance," he says, clearly annoyed that we're being disturbed. He turns away from me and reaches for his phone, opening an app showing a woman pounding on his front door.

"I hate to break it to you, but I don't share my things either, so she might want to think twice before walking into this house."

His eyes burn into mine before he drops a kiss on my lips. "Keep saying things like that, and I'll let her up here so you can ride my cock in front of her just to prove your point." He stands up, and my eyes shamelessly drag over his inked, muscular body as he slips on his underwear. "But if I don't answer this, she'll never go away. Trust me."

"Jesus, she's the ex, isn't she?"

"Client, Sydney. And if you call her anything else, I'm pretty sure my dick might fall off. Then what will you do?"

"I guess I'll have to ride those thick fingers that know just how to get me off." He freezes halfway through slipping on a white T-shirt.

"Fuck baby, you are just... I don't even have the words for you right now," he says, letting out a breathless laugh as he shakes his head in disbelief.

His eyes linger on me for a split second before he turns and walks out of the room, leaving the door wide open behind him. The sound of his footsteps fades, but the charged air between us remains.

While he's gone, I quickly search for my underwear. Muffled voices rise from the level below me, but Edison's house is ridiculously large, and I can't make out a single word. The sound of someone running up the stairs cuts through my silence, and I climb back onto the bed, hoping it's Edison, but the sound of heels tells me otherwise.

Suddenly, a woman bursts into the room, and my jaw almost drops.

Oh my god, she's famous.

However, as soon as she flings my dress at me with a sneer, the initial shock of her standing before me fades away, replaced by a version of me who is ready to rip out her terrible hair extensions and strangle her with them.

"I don't care what he's paying you. Get out."

Edison steps in right behind her, his face contorting with barely contained anger. "Get out of my fucking house, Maddy."

"Get her out!" she screams back at him, pointing in my direction.

"Yeah, I'm not going anywhere," I say with a laugh while holding my ground.

"Do you know who I am? I could crush you."

"You're a low-budget actress who can't do anything to me, and I honestly don't give a shit who you are or how many straight-to-TV movies you've done."

My words hang in the air, and I watch her face twist in anger. I glance behind her, and there's Edison with that smirk of his, one arm draped around his waist, while his hand rubs his jaw and a flicker of amusement crosses his face at how unfiltered I am.

"Are you going to let her talk to me like that, Edison?"

"Yeah, pretty much," he replies, and just like that, he somehow got even hotter. "Where are Ace and Drew?"

"They're outside. I didn't tell them I was coming here because they would've called you." Her whole vibe suddenly shifts, and I can tell something's off. Her expression softens, and a fake-as-shit sadness creeps into her eyes. "I'm paying *you* to help me. Please, I really need to talk to you alone."

"Schedule a meeting with Lee. I've already told you that I don't do this anymore."

"But it's me, Edison. You know me. Please, I came to you because we have history and I'm comfortable with you," she whines, her voice so annoyingly pitiful that I can't help but roll my eyes.

I watch Edison closely, knowing that this is where things between us could get messy.

"You lost the right to me or my time when you sucked off your director, Maddy."

Oh Jesus, is he bitter? Maybe that's why he hates her, or maybe he doesn't—maybe she hurt him.

"I know I made mistakes, but so did you, and now I have to see this whore in your bed."

Edison's eyes instantly darken, and his body becomes rigid. "The woman in my bed has already given me more in the short time we've known each other than you ever did throughout our entire relationship. Now for the final time, get out of my damn house."

She whips her head toward me and sneers. "Enjoy him while you can. You're just another blonde to keep him entertained until he gets bored and remembers who should be warming his bed."

"Out, Maddy!" This time, he yells—really yells—his voice echoing through the room, but she doesn't even flinch, like his outburst didn't faze her at all.

My favorite red flag just showed up flashing green, and I'm here for it.

Maybe he's been green all along.

"Besides, look at you. You're a nobody. Edison likes women who are on his level, and by the looks of it, you're so beneath him that he must've really been in a desperate place when he found you."

"I've never put my hands on a woman, but I swear to god, Maddy, you're testing my fucking limits."

"I'm leaving now, Edison, and I'll let you deal with this, but just remember that I love you, and I'm not giving up. I'm here to fight for you."

"I thought you were here because you needed my help."

"I am, but seeing you again made me realize that getting you back is just as important." She brushes past him, her presence feeling too close, too invasive—but maybe I'm the one who shouldn't be here.

I don't want to be that person—the one who allows someone else's bullshit to get under their skin—but her words are digging deeper than I'd like to admit.

"Give me a second. I don't trust her to actually leave." He trails after her, but he's only gone for a moment. When he returns to the room, he sits down beside me on the bed.

"I'm sorry about that, Sydney."

"It's fine."

"No, it isn't. I didn't plan on having any baggage, but somehow, it found me anyway."

"We all carry baggage, Edison."

"Do you?" he asks, his eyes searching mine.

"Only emotionally. You won't find a crazy ex blowing up my phone or barging in when you're half-naked in my bed anytime soon."

He hovers over me, his lips just grazing the swell of my breasts. "You still want me in your bed?" he asks, but I hear the uncertainty in his voice, and for the first time, I sense a crack in his confidence. "Promise me you won't listen to anything she said. I really like you, and I don't want that low-budget actress ruining what's going on here between us." We both burst into laughter as he effortlessly lightens the mood. "So... can I still come over for Thai and fuck you all over your apartment?"

"You'd better. I need you to make me come at least once more before you leave me to find your next blonde."

"What if I said I didn't want another blonde, brunette, redhead, or any other hair color?"

For a moment, I can't find my voice.

He isn't talking about a preference.

He's talking about me.

He wants me.

"Then I would say you don't know me well enough to decide that."

"I know enough," he whispers hoarsely. "I know what I feel, and this connection is more... so much more than anything I've felt before." He dips his head to place a kiss on my bare stomach before he slides his hand over the curve of my breasts and threads his fingers through my hair. "Is it only me who feels this way, Sydney?"

Meeting someone is the easy part. Even falling in love comes naturally to most people. However, finding someone who sparks your soul? That shit is rare, and deep down, I know I don't want to push this man away.

"No, it's not just you."

"Then I need you to ignore everything she said because you're exactly who I've been waiting for."

Chapter 14

Sydney

"Has he asked you yet?" Cora tilts her head, her curious eyes peering over the rim of her coffee mug.

"No, and I don't expect him to."

"You've been like the ghost of Christmas past for the last two weeks. Trust me, he's going to ask you to spend the holiday with him."

Edison and I have been practically inseparable, spending every waking hour together when neither of us is working. It's intense, but it doesn't feel overwhelming—it feels right. Like I'm meant to be close to him.

"I give great head. That's all it is." My attempt at deflecting fails, and I know it because my beautiful best friend is fucking relentless and sees right through me.

"Please. If that's all it was, he wouldn't look at you like you're the reason the sky sparkles at night."

"Alright, I know you're all about the love, but let's tone it down a little."

"You can deny it all you want, but that man is so gone for you."

It's been two weeks since Edison's ex-girlfriend branded me a whore, then he went ahead and fucked me like one. We've been in each other's beds every night since, like two lust-drunk teenagers who can't get enough of each other. And the sex—my god, the sex—has left me utterly ruined for anyone else.

I've always taken the lead in bed with my previous partners, thinking I had to if I ever wanted to get what I needed, but it turns out I've just been with the wrong men. Where I once had to demand what my body craved, now I don't have to say a word. Edison knows exactly how to get me off, and he loves nothing more than to take control, which I'm happy to give him.

Two weeks isn't a long time, but it's natural to grow close when you've spent as much time together as we have. But it's not just about the sex. Sure, he's had me in every position imaginable, and there isn't a single place in my apartment that I haven't been fucked over, on, or against, but it's more than that. He touches me like it's the first time, every time, and he kisses me like it could be his last breath, and honestly, I've never felt more adored.

The way he listens to every word I say is something I'm still trying to get used to. When I talk, he never has his phone in his hand and never glances away like he's getting bored. Instead, he gives me his full attention, like every word I say matters to him. And even though he looks at me like I'm crazy and tells me he's doing the bare minimum, I have to explain to him that the world we live in now has people more detached than ever.

I'm falling in love with him, and that scares the living shit out of me. Edison is the kind of guy who, once you give him your heart, you'll never get it back—even if he decides he doesn't want it anymore.

"When he asks, don't run from him. You've got a shot at happiness, so take it," Cora presses, urging me to get out of my own way and not let fear mess this up.

"Says the woman who's taken nearly two weeks to go on a date with the guy she's been obsessing over for months."

"I did not obsess," she says with a playful smile, but I raise an eyebrow, and she laughs. "Okay, maybe a little."

"If you had listened to me months ago, you and Nick could've been married by now."

"Please, my wedding will need at least a year to plan." She chuckles, bringing her mug to her lips with a grin. "And besides, I was never going to make the first move."

"Why not? You're gorgeous, and you're my favorite person in the world. Nobody in their right mind would turn you down."

"You have to say that!" She laughs, her eyes crinkling at the corners.

I hear the door swing open, and a blast of cold air sweeps through the café as an elderly couple steps inside, hand in hand.

"It doesn't make it any less true," I add, watching as her attention turns to them.

"What can I get you?" Cora asks, and the elderly couple share a look—a silent conversation that comes from years of shared moments and knowing each other inside and out.

"Two hot chocolates, please," the woman says as her husband wraps an arm around her and rubs her shoulder to try and warm her up.

I find myself drawn to them. The way he looks at her when she isn't watching, and the way her smile reaches her eyes when she turns to face him melts me where I stand. I don't need to know them to see that they have the kind of love that's built over time, and maybe having someone there holding your hand after all the years and changes isn't such a bad thing after all.

A few hours later, I'm wandering around the club, feeling like an idiot in this lame-ass festive getup we've all been forced—because, let's be real, it wasn't exactly optional—to wear until Christmas is over. If I didn't already feel uncomfortable being here tonight, this outfit is really pushing it. I'm rocking bright-green stockings with tiny bells that jingle with every step, candy cane pattern underwear that barely counts as clothing, and to top it off, a fucking Santa hat perched on top of my head. I look like some messed-up love child of an elf, Santa, and a holiday candy store all rolled into one mortifying package, and I want to die of embarrassment.

But as the night drags on, I hate being here more and more. Scratch that—as the weeks go on, it's becoming unbearable.

Every look from a guy that reveals all the perverted thoughts running through his mind makes my skin crawl. The way they stare at me, like they're imagining doing things I would rather chop off my own arms than go along with, is enough to make me nauseous. And every word that leaves my mouth when I'm forced to talk to these assholes—whose inflated egos are just a cover for their micropenises—makes me want to cut out my own tongue. The things that I used to brush off are now the ones that weigh on me, and they're getting harder to ignore.

And it's all because of that mountain of a man who's bulldozed his way into my heart, despite it being sealed tight with what I thought was an impenetrable lock.

Get out of my head, Edison.

Yet he's always there, filling every corner of my mind, always pulling me deeper into this feeling.

Maybe it's because he's not here tonight.

Usually, he shows up when I'm working. He knows I find it easier to get through a night of putting on the act I've perfected when I can find his eyes across the room. It makes a difference knowing I can slip away for a moment just to hear his voice, feel the promise in his words, and be sure that the second I get out of here, his hands will be all over my body, grounding me and reminding me that I'm only his.

The only thing I enjoy now about being here is when I get to dance for him. Which we've now agreed is only ever for him, no matter how many pairs of eyes are on me.

"Are you okay, Sydney?" I'm snapped out of my thoughts by Coco—whose real name is actually Melinda. She somehow manages to look both ridiculous and gorgeous in her little Miss Santa getup.

"I'm fine, thank you."

"You sure? You don't seem yourself tonight."

"Rough day, but thank you for checking in," I reply with a forced smile. "Actually, could you cover me for a minute? I just need to take a breather."

"Sure, take as long as you need."

I leave the club's main area and head down the dark hallway that leads to the reserved rooms. The purple lights barely illuminate the space around me, making it harder to see further down the corridor. It's always quiet down here, giving me the moment of solitude I need to try and get my shit together.

I lean against the cold wall and tilt my head back as I release a long breath, trying to steady the storm twisting in my mind.

The thoughts in my head are suffocating.

Edison. The club. The way I'm being pulled in two different directions—one toward the life I know, safe and predictable, and the other toward the guy who's stolen my heart and completely wrecked my sense of control.

Get it together, Sydney.

Heavy footsteps echo down the hallway, forcing me to stand up straight, and my muscles tense as I go on high alert. Men aren't allowed down here unless they're accompanied by one of the girls, so whoever is here is breaking the club rules—unless it's security or Ash, which I'm certain it's not. My heart pounds as I force myself to slip back into character, pushing off the wall when the steps get louder as they get closer.

When a silhouette finally appears, my guard crumbles, and the tension that had my muscles coiled tight disappears, replaced by a surge of warmth that rushes through my veins.

"I'm not exactly thrilled about you being down here alone, Sydney."

"Would you rather I was down here with somebody else?"

"Not a chance."

My heart races, and my stomach tightens as I reach for him, fingers curling into the lapels of his jacket. He effortlessly pins me against the wall, his body pressing into mine, trapping me in place. His lips hover just above my jaw, teasing me with the warmth of his breath as he leans in closer.

"You missed me, baby?" he asks, his voice a low, seductive drawl.

"Too much."

"I could tell."

"What do you mean?" He tilts his head back slightly, his eyes locking onto mine as he looks down at me.

"I've been watching you tonight, even though you couldn't see me."

"All night?" I suddenly feel vulnerable but not weak—just exposed. "Why?"

"Two reasons, baby. The first is that I hate being in a place where you're not," he whispers, pressing his lips against my forehead. "The second reason is that I wanted to be sure you'd be fine here without me like you used to be."

"I don't think I am okay, and I don't know why."

"Are you sure about that?" His steel eyes find mine again. "You see, I think you do know why, and I want you to tell me."

I swallow hard, but I don't stop my truth from leaving me. "I hate being here. I hate anyone looking at me like I'm not..."

"Not mine?" he questions, his voice carrying a dark edge. I nod slowly, and his hand captures my chin in his grasp. "You know exactly who you belong to, baby."

"They don't care. Nobody in there gives a shit."

"Fuck everyone else." His hand cradles my jaw, pulling me in as his lips claim mine. When he finally pulls back, his voice is calm but firm. "It's just a job, baby. You don't have to keep doing this. I know it means nothing to you."

"It's how I make a living. It's how I take care of myself." I trail my fingers across Edison's chest, teasing the open button at the top of his black shirt.

"You've built walls so high, Sydney, that anyone would have to be out of their damn mind to even try and climb them. But I'm here, baby. I climbed them, and now I want to take care of you in every sense of the word."

"I know what you're getting at, and I don't want that. You know I don't."

"Yeah, you're little Miss Independent. I get it," he says, as his fingers trail a slow, possessive path down the curve between my breasts. "And as sexy as I find that, I still can't help but want to look after you." He places gentle kisses along my shoulder. "God, you're such a distraction in this outfit," he whispers against my skin as his hands slide over my hips before gripping my ass.

"I look ridiculous." I laugh, and I hear a deep chuckle escape him.

"You look..." He steps back slightly, and his eyes roam over every inch of my body and the festive fuckup that's covering it. "Okay, I get why you hate it, but all I can think about is hearing you jingle while I'm inside you."

I playfully slap a hand against his chest, but before I can pull away, he catches it and brushes his lips against the inside of my wrist.

"Can you please get me out of here? I really need to be alone with you, away from this place," I whisper as I slide my hands over his chest, feeling the hard muscle beneath his shirt.

He leans in, resting his forehead against mine. "Yeah, I can do that."

I press a kiss to his jaw, feeling the slight roughness of his stubble against my lips before dragging my tongue along the black phoenix tattoo on his neck. I hear him exhale, his breath catching as he melts into my touch, his entire body relaxing as if it's the only thing keeping him grounded.

In moments like this, in these stolen seconds, I realize how much I've changed. I don't know the exact moment I became this person—this needy, vulnerable version of myself, one who's so completely wrapped up in him—but I don't care.

All that matters is the way we feel together.

The way we just *fit*.

I can't ever remember fitting with anyone like this.

"Let me go get changed, and I'll meet you out front."

"Okay, but if you don't hurry up, I'll haul your ass out of here like a caveman."

"Now that I would love to see."

"Try me," he says with a smirk, stepping back slightly before taking my hand in his.

He leads me back to the dressing room, his hand wrapped around mine. As we reach the door, he stops and leans in, placing a soft kiss on my forehead. When he turns and walks away, I can't help but find myself drawn in, watching the way he moves, and only when he's out of sight do I finally slip inside the room.

God, it's like fucking Insta-love. I'm a walking trope.

I move over to where I hung the clothes I arrived in. Just as my fingers brush the fabric, an unmistakable voice cuts through the air.

Maddy hisses behind me, her voice dripping with venom. "So you really are a dirty little whore." I spin around to face her—Edison's ex—her eyes glinting with a sick kind of satisfaction. "You know, I really thought this was going to be a challenge. I thought you might be hard to get rid of, especially with how Edison acted that morning. But look at you." Her cruel, mocking laughter fills the space between us, bouncing off the walls and slamming into my ears.

As her judgy eyes rake over me, I don't even need to glance down at myself to know how exposed I am. For the first time ever, the usual fire inside me—the stubborn side of me that won't let anybody tear me down—has completely vanished and been replaced with something that feels way too much like shame.

"What do you want?" I ask, my voice coming out steadier than I feel.

"I want to talk."

"Well, if you could hurry it up, that would be great. I have a guy I'm pretty desperate to get back to."

"My guy," she states firmly, her voice filled with conviction like she actually believes it.

The fire inside me, dulled by the shock of her fucking audacity, flares back to life. Call me possessive, but I couldn't care less. When it comes to him, I am—completely, unapologetically.

"Is that seriously what you think?" I ask, a laugh escaping me before I can stop it. "Even if I weren't around, he still wouldn't want you."

"Deep down, you must know you're not the right woman for him." I shake my head, still laughing at her delusions. "I mean, how could you be? Just look at you." She points at me, and a cruel smile spreads across her face, clearly trying to make me feel as worthless as she thinks I am.

"If Edison wanted you, he'd be with you. I'm sure you're aware of how persistent he is."

"Yeah, but I also know he gets bored easily. Although he never did with me. He only left me because I made a mistake."

"Are you done?"

"No," she snaps. "Maybe you should ask him why he was still sleeping with me just a few months ago if you're so sure I'm not what he wants." I take a deep breath and rub the space between my eyebrows, trying to stop my inner bitch from smashing the nearest mirror with her heavily botoxed face. "You're not good enough for him, and you know it."

Okay, that one stung a little.

"He's a powerful man with a lot of money. He commands respect, especially in his business, and has an image to uphold. Do you honestly believe he'll get serious with someone whose pussy is practically hanging out and who spreads herself to men for money?" Angry tears threaten to consume me as her words hit just where she intended. "He'll either force you to quit your job, or he'll leave you because I guarantee there's a part of him that's embarrassed that his girlfriend is this." She gestures toward me once again, her eyes sweeping over me with disgust. She thinks I'm beneath him. "He deserves a woman he can actually be proud of, and you're not it. So do him a favor—let him go before he breaks your heart and you ruin his reputation."

The fight inside me still flickers, but her judgment is suffocating.

Chapter 15

Edison

I haven't taken my eyes off Sydney all night. The love of my goddamn life has been walking around, looking completely lost among a sea of men whose thoughts were so loud, so predatory, that it took everything in me not to end every single one of them.

I knew she didn't want to be at the club tonight, and it gnawed at me. The unease in her eyes, the way she moved—everything about her was silently screaming that she'd rather be anywhere else. If she loved this job, then I would want her to stay for as long as she could, to keep doing what makes her happy.

Do I like it? Hell no. I'd be lying if I said otherwise, but it's not because of her. Because, fuck me, watching her walk around in those sinful little outfits all night, knowing I'm the one who gets to tear it off her, makes me so fucking hard. But what I can't tolerate—what grates on my shit—is anyone else looking at her, even for a split second, with the delusion that they'll ever hear the way her voice breaks when she comes, thinking they'll ever know how phenomenal it feels to be inside her.

That's mine.

Every sound she makes—every breathless moan—belongs to me.

That's my privilege.

My claim.

There's no denying that I'm possessive of her, but when you find the one person who makes your entire universe make sense, who doesn't just cross your mind but who lives in it, you don't let go.

I'm a jealous son of a bitch when it comes to Sydney, and I refuse to hide it.

I know why she doesn't want to be here tonight. I can see it so clearly. It's our connection—it's messing with her head, twisting things around, and I hate seeing her so lost. She needs to understand that she has me in every way. I'm hers, no question about it. No matter what happens or what she decides to do, I'm not going anywhere. Finding her was like coming home—like her heart was built just for me.

After reluctantly pulling myself away from her, I head toward my car. However, as I get closer, a flash of movement catches my attention—a few of my guys hanging around near the club's side entrance, tucked into the shadows.

"Drew?" I call out, and the Viking-looking beast of a man standing before me spins around. "What are you doing here? You've been assigned to Maddy, haven't you?" My eyes narrow as I try to read the situation. Drew isn't one to leave his post without a damn good reason, so the fact that he's here, away from where he's supposed to be, sets off alarms in my head.

"She made us bring her here, boss."

"Maddy's in there?" My voice tightens as my heart begins to pound so hard that it feels like it's about to break through my chest.

"She's been in there for about an hour now," Drew says, his tone steady but laced with the concern that I know matches my face. "She told us to let her go through the back and wait for her here."

A fucking hour!

I don't bother answering. I just spin on my heel and head straight back into the club. My mind is only focused on one thing—finding my girl, and she'd better be exactly where I left her.

Chapter 16

Sydney

Maddy's spewing poison like someone who's used to always getting what they want. It goes beyond bitterness—it's a toxic entitlement that runs deep, fueling her need to claim ownership over Edison.

I know exactly what she's trying to do to me. She wants to tear me down and make me feel so bad about myself that I break under her words. However, I refuse to give her that satisfaction. But that doesn't mean some of what she said doesn't hurt because it does.

Whatever Edison did before me is none of my business—that's his past. But what pisses me off is that she got to throw it in my face.

I know Edison is highly regarded. That's how he's become so successful and why everyone wants what his company has to offer. I'm also fully aware that what I do is looked down upon by a lot of ignorant people. However, he's never once made me feel ashamed of what I do, nor has he ever made me feel like he's embarrassed of me in any way.

It's not him—it's my own feelings that are shifting, making me question things I never used to doubt. Maddy's words aren't getting to me because they actually mean anything. It's because she's poking at insecurities I wasn't really aware I had.

"You know everything I'm saying is true," she says, her voice cold and cutting as she flips her golden hair over her shoulder. "Just let him go so he can find someone he can actually call his wife—someone who could be his children's mother someday. Because you must know it can never be you, right?"

Her intent is to make me doubt everything I have with him, to make me question what I mean to him, but I refuse to let her undermine what we have and what I feel.

"And you think that's you?"

"Sweetie, I know it's me."

"Are you insane?" I snap, my patience now wearing really fucking thin. "I'm genuinely curious if you're actually crazy because it seems like you truly believe your own bullshit." Her eyes narrow, and I see a flicker of fury flash across her face, but I don't back down. "You know what? Maybe he and I won't be together for the rest of our lives, but I'm exactly what he wants right now. Not some stupid bitch who cheats on a guy as beautiful as Edison just to get a better role because she doesn't have enough talent to earn it any other way." Her face contorts with rage, and I see the sting my words have left behind.

Good. Let it burn.

"You don't fucking know me!" she shouts, her voice going shrill, but I don't even bother looking back as I stride toward the door.

I'm still wearing this ridiculous mix of festive lingerie I've been stuck in all night, and the tiny bells jingle with every step.

As I open the door, I come face-to-face with Edison, standing before me with that powerful, commanding presence that always sets me on edge. His thunderous eyes scan me from head to toe, and his chest heaves as if he's been running—or fighting to get to me.

"Where is she?"

I tilt my head back, gesturing toward the space behind me where Maddy stands. His eyes flick past me, and his jaw tightens as they find her.

"Let me in," he demands, his tone leaving no room for argument. I widen the door and step aside, feeling the heat radiating off his body as he brushes past me.

"What are you doing here, Maddy?" he asks calmly, but it feels almost too calm.

"Why are you here? With her, with someone like this," Maddy spits in disgust.

I take a few steps back, ready to turn and leave so they can hash this out when Edison's voice booms out across the room. "Don't fucking move, Sydney."

"Edison..."

"I mean it. Don't move."

"Let her go. This is between us," Maddy insists, which is pretty fucking ironic considering she was the one waiting in here to ambush me.

Edison looks at me, his gaze softening just a touch as he says, "Stay. You're going to need to hear this." I nod in response, and he turns back to face the psycho in front of us.

"I thought you had more respect for yourself than this, Edison," she says with a sneer, her voice slicing through the room. "Unlike the tramp who's been in your bed."

"How did you do it, Maddy?" he asks, not even flinching at her insults.

"Do what?"

"Blind me," he says as he takes slow, deliberate steps toward her. "How did you pull together evidence so convincing that I had no choice but to believe your stalker was real?"

What the hell?

This is the first time I've seen this side of Edison. I know he's intense, but this—this is something else entirely. There's a darkness in him, a carefully leashed fury simmering just beneath the surface, twisting through those storm-filled eyes.

Trying to read him feels impossible; it's like he's slipped behind a wall only he can see through, leaving me on the other side.

"I didn't, Edison, I swear."

"Maddy, if you ever want me to trust you, this is the only chance you're going to get," he warns.

My eyes narrow as I watch them, trying to figure out what's unfolding between them and the unspoken history that's rising to the surface.

"Edison," she whispers, her voice shaking as tears pool in her eyes, but it's impossible to miss the guilt etched into every line of her face. Whatever she used to suck Edison in was nothing but manipulation.

"Come on, Mads. I know you're here for me, but you know I'll never give us another chance if it starts with a lie."

A rush of emotions hits me all at once as my back meets the door, the impact grounding me as my mind races. Every instinct is screaming at me to run, to get the hell out of this room, but I can't tear my eyes away from them. I stand there, frozen, watching as he softens to the woman he swore he hated—the woman he said meant nothing to him.

The way he looks at her now, like she means everything to him, shatters something inside me. I try to breathe through the pounding in my chest as my heart slams against my ribs.

He's got to be playing her—he has to be. Because what we have is the most real thing I've ever felt in my life.

"Talk to me, Maddy."

"I'm sorry, Edison, I'm so sorry," she cries out, her voice cracking with desperation. "I just needed a way in. I needed a way to get back to you." She steps into his body, gripping his shoulders while his hands remain firmly in his pockets. "I was desperate for you. Do you understand that? There's nothing I wouldn't do for you. Nothing."

All I can do now is focus on him—his reaction to her.

The way in which she clings to him as if he were her lifeline while he stands there, completely unreadable, is driving me out of my damn mind.

I have no idea what's happening here, but the feeling that I might lose him is twisting in my gut like a knife. The thought alone makes me want to tear down walls, grab him by the shoulders, and shake him until he understands exactly what he's risking—what he's throwing away.

But I don't.

Instead, I stand here, frozen, watching this beautiful disaster play out before me, practically handing him the match while he sets fire to everything we built.

"How did you do it? Tell me," he asks, his tone softer now.

Her hands slowly slide from his shoulders, lingering until they come to rest on his chest as if she's searching for a way to get closer to him.

"I spent a long time with you. I know how your company works and what boxes need to be checked for you and the cops to take this seriously," she confesses, her voice shaky.

Edison exhales deeply, tilting his head back to stare at the ceiling as if he's searching for some way to make sense of all this—like he doesn't know what the hell to do right now.

"Please forgive me. I only did it because of how much I still love you," she continues, tears spilling down her cheeks.

I'll give this bitch some credit—she can really push those crocodile tears out. But the second Edison reaches out and wraps his arms around her, something sharp and hot erupts inside me.

Anger.

Betrayal.

Like how the earth is bound to the sun—one can't exist without the other, and right now, it feels like our star has imploded.

So fine.

Let him blow it all to hell if that's what he wants. If he's that ready to destroy it, then maybe he was never worth my gravity in the first place.

Chapter 17

Edison

I can feel every ounce of Sydney's energy shift as I stand here, holding Maddy close.

The air thickens with her hurt and confusion, and I can practically taste the bitterness of her emotions in the back of my throat.

The woman who makes my skin crawl has her hands on me, her fingers digging into me like poison, while the woman I love stands there, her face etched with doubt. Everything we've been building—the trust I've worked my ass off to earn—is beginning to unravel, and I can feel her slipping through my fingers.

I despise this woman in front of me. First, for deceiving me—something I figured out the second I knew she was here—and for making me look like a goddamn idiot in front of my employees because I believed she was in trouble.

I don't make errors. Ever.

But she played me so well that I stupidly let my guard down and didn't suspect a thing.

But what really pisses me off is the way she's made Sydney feel—I don't even need to look at my girl to know she's drowning in the belief that I'm betraying her.

It's okay, baby. I'm yours. Just give me time.

"I've missed you, Edison. I've missed you so much."

"I know," I reply, smoothing down her hair and focusing on the dry, coarse texture—nothing like Sydney's; her hair glides through my fingers like silk and looks even better wrapped around my fist.

"Wow," Sydney says, a shocked laugh escaping her lips. "You need to leave now. Before I call security."

She's not just hurt—she's fucking furious.

"Baby, I own the security." She shoots me a glare, hating me right now, but I know that'll change as soon as I can get close to her. Reluctantly, I shift my gaze from Sydney to the woman who repulses me. "Give me a second to speak with her, Maddy."

"I can hear you, asshole," Sydney snaps, and I bite back a laugh, knowing my feisty, strong, take-no-shit girl is probably thinking up the most creative way to rip off my balls right now. And, honestly, I wouldn't blame her.

I pull away from Maddy and turn to Sydney, but she won't even look at me. Her eyes are fixed on anything but mine, clearly trying to shut me out. I take a few steps closer, reaching for her, but she backs up even further against the door, putting as much distance between us as possible.

I close the gap, pressing my body against hers, feeling the tension rolling off her like electricity in the air.

I lean in, my mouth brushing against her ear. The heat of my breath is all I have to shatter the wall she's desperately trying to build.

"I'm sorry." Finally, her eyes lift to mine, and I see them glazed over.

"Don't you dare say another word to me."

"Trust me, baby. I need you to trust me," I whisper, my voice low and desperate, almost broken, as I try to hold onto my girl.

When I pull back, I feel everything between us—every second I've craved her, every charged moment that's sparked between us, every breath we've stolen together—I see the woman I've fallen head over fucking heels for, the one who's torn me open in ways I never imagined.

I reach behind her to lock the door, and a soft click seals us in the room. My hand slides down to hers, guiding it as I press my back against the door, pulling Sydney tightly against me, her back flush to my chest.

"What are you doing?" Maddy asks, her voice edged with confusion, and now she's the one who looks lost.

"I need you to pay close attention and listen very carefully to me, Maddy."

I drag my fingers slowly up and down Sydney's bare arms, getting high off her scent and the warmth of her skin beneath my fingertips.

"How long were we together? A few months?" I ask, my focus shifting entirely to Sydney, letting Maddy feel the shift in the air and the way the energy between us crackles. I want her to see it. I want her to see us and feel what we share.

Sydney's breath hitches, and I know she can feel it too—our unbreakable connection that's been there from the start. I want Maddy to understand just how little those months meant to me compared to what I've found now.

Because there's no going back.

Not for me.

Not for us.

"It was almost a year," she snaps, the fake tears now long gone.

"A year, right," I say, gathering Sydney's long platinum hair, brushing it over one side, and letting it cascade down her chest. I drop my mouth to her exposed shoulder, feeling her shudder as my lips graze her skin, a tremor that shoots straight to my dick. "Do you know..." I murmur, my breath warm on my girl's skin, "the day I met Sydney, I felt more of a connection with her in those first few seconds than I did with you throughout our entire relationship."

"You're a liar. You're just trying to hurt me."

"I'd have to care about you to want to hurt you, and I don't."

As I cup her throat, Sydney's head tilts back, giving me the perfect angle to drag my tongue along the curve of her ear. I hold her tight against me, feeling her melt and tense all at once.

"You know what else I don't care about?" I continue, locking eyes with Maddy, who looks like she's ready to start spitting fire. "What this beautiful woman does for a living because I know I'm the only one for her." I let my hand drift down Sydney's chest, fingers tracing over her soft skin until I reach the waistband of her panties. "While you really were anyone's, Maddy."

"What do you expect when you made me feel so unwanted?" she says, as if she actually believes that lie.

"Deep down, you were never what I wanted. Clearly, you picked up on that faster than I did."

This isn't about getting revenge on Maddy. I prefer to call it returning the favor.

She hurt someone I love. Now, I'm going to hurt her.

"If I ever realized I could feel this way, I would've left you and gone looking for her a hell of a lot sooner."

I tilt Sydney's face to mine, and my thumb grazes her jaw as I draw her closer. Green eyes meet mine, and I hold her gaze, letting her see every raw, unapologetic emotion coursing through me before my hand slides back down to her throat, my fingers spreading wide to cradle her neck.

"Let me out of this room right now, Edison," Maddy almost snarls, yet all I can do is laugh. A dark, low rumble bubbles up from deep inside me, exposing me as the sadistic bastard I feel like being right now.

"Why the hell would I do that when you've been waiting in here half the night?" I taunt while slipping my fingers into the waistband of Sydney's underwear. "You've been waiting in here, ready to manipulate her, ready to break her down and make her feel less than she is, all because you're a spoiled little bitch who doesn't like the word no."

I turn my attention back to Sydney, stroking the side of her face with my thumb. "Baby?" I whisper, watching her closely. Her eyes darken when they collide with mine, creating a shadow of desire that makes my pulse quicken and my cock harden. "Can I touch you?" Her teeth graze her lower lip, a slight hesitation that only makes my blood burn hotter, and then she nods, giving herself over to me completely.

My lips collide with hers as my hand slides lower, finding her already slick and ready. I pull back, my gaze fixed on hers, close enough to see every flicker of emotion that dances across her face—the way her eyes flutter shut briefly, the way her mouth parts with a desperate sigh. But right now, I'm focused, watching her closely, searching for the slightest hint of uncertainty. If there's a moment where she looks uncomfortable, I'll stop without a second thought. However, all I see and feel from her is trust—pure, intoxicating trust.

"Eyes forward, Sydney."

"Let me out before I call the cops and tell them you're holding me against my will," Maddy spits out.

"Call them. I dare you. I'm sure they'd love to hear how you wasted their time with your fake stalker story," I reply, a smirk tugging at my lips.

I continue running the pad of my middle finger over Sydney's clit, circling it slowly in the way that I know drives her fucking wild.

"You wouldn't."

"Trust me, I would. I'll also release everything else I have on you—every dirty secret you'd hate for the world to find out." Sydney grips my arm, her nails digging into my skin—a clear sign she's getting close. "Now shut up, Maddy, and watch what I look like when I'm falling in love with someone."

"Edison," Sydney rasps out.

"You're doing so well, beautiful," I whisper, my lips brushing against her ear. She raises an arm, wrapping it around my neck as her swollen clit pulses under my touch. I can feel her losing herself to the pleasure I'm bringing her, but I'm not ready for this to be over so soon.

I slow my movements, and her fingers tighten in my hair—a needy grip that has me smirking. She lets out a frustrated whimper, her body arching into mine as I slide a finger inside her. The way she instantly clenches around me, her pussy silently begging for more, has my dick throbbing in my pants, desperate to feel that same heat wrapped around me.

"You've made your point, Edison," Maddy growls, yet despite the disgust etched on her face, she doesn't look away.

"When you see what making her come does to me, then I'll have made my point," I bite out, dragging my finger slowly over Sydney's clit, coating her in her arousal.

As I start to rub again, she presses herself against my hand, her movements desperate and unrestrained, her body responding in a way that only I can draw out of her.

"Tell her, baby," I urge, my voice low and commanding. "Tell her exactly who I belong to."

"Me," she pants out, "you belong to me."

"That's right, baby. I'm yours. Now give it up to me."

Sydney detonates seconds later, her pussy pulsing as a broken cry escapes her lips, and she shatters in my arms. I hold her tight against my chest as her limbs go slack, and like a prayer, my name spills from her mouth. I grip her chin, guiding her gaze to mine, holding her there for just a beat before closing the distance. There's nothing gentle in the way I kiss her—just raw, overpowering hunger.

"That's my girl," I whisper, feeling nothing but pride and a desperate-as-fuck need to get back inside her.

"Well, you've changed," Maddy spits out bitterly.

I don't bother looking at her. My eyes stay fixed on the blonde beauty in my arms, the one who I would walk through fire for. My focus is entirely on Sydney—her flushed cheeks, her soft labored breaths, the way her body still trembles against mine. Maddy's anger is nothing but distant noise compared to what's unfolding between us.

"The right person will do that to you," I say unapologetically. "Now, if you'll excuse us."

"Don't even think about walking out of that door, Edison!" she screams.

"If you ever come near either of us again, I'll unleash everything I have on you, and trust me, it's far more than you realize. I will fucking destroy you without even blinking. Do you understand?" She holds my stare, searching for any hint that I might be bluffing. But I watch as the realization settles in, her jaw tightening, and a shadow crosses her eyes. She gives me a grudging nod, lips pressed into a thin line as if she's swallowing glass, before turning her glare to Sydney with an unmistakable look of disgust.

"Go ahead, call me a whore again—because it's this *whore* who owns his heart. Not you. Never you." Sydney spits out, and the fire in her eyes makes me ache to kiss her again.

I turn and unlock the door, and all I can think about is getting Sydney away from this crazy bitch.

The moment we step into the dimly lit hallway, I scoop her up into my arms, and she clings to me like she needs this closeness just as much as I do. However, there's a thick silence between us, heavy with what just went down in that room. I don't let go of her for a second, holding her firmly against me as I push through the back of the club.

As we approach the car, I spot Drew still lingering outside, his posture now tense as he waits for my instruction. Without slowing down, I call out to him, "You're off the job. Tell the others, and get home to your wives." He nods and turns away to relay the message to the rest of my guys.

I unlock my car and swing the door open, still holding Sydney close to me. The cold air bites at her exposed skin, and I feel her shiver against me.

"Jesus, you must be freezing." I carefully set her down in the passenger seat, and without a second thought, I shrug off my jacket and drape it over her shoulders. "Here, baby, take this." I pull the fabric tight around her before tucking a strand of her hair behind her ear.

"Thank you; I'm okay though," she whispers. "I just want to go home." I press a quick kiss to her forehead before closing the door and heading around to the driver's side.

"I need to warm this car up," I say as I settle into the seat.

I reach for the ignition, but before I can turn the key, her fingers glide across my arm, grounding me as I feel myself begin to spiral. I'm caught up in my head, worrying about how she feels about what just went down. However, her touch reminds me that she's here, she's with me, and no matter what happens, nothing will come between us.

"I promise I'm okay," she says, trying to calm the storm she knows is brewing inside me.

Chapter 18

Sydney

The drive back to my apartment was quiet, but the silence was heavy, almost suffocating, and Edison's thoughts were loud enough to fill the car. He kept shifting in his seat, his fingers tapping restlessly against the steering wheel and his jaw clenched in a way that showed me how quickly his mind was racing.

I got caught up in the moment back there—the heat, the possessiveness, the way he looked at me like he would burn the club down if it meant keeping me close. But now, with the adrenaline wearing off and the reality sinking in, a knot of uncertainty curls in my stomach.

I know he's worried—not about what happened, but about me and what this means for us. And for someone who never loses his cool, he's sure as hell looked rattled ever since we left the club.

We walk into my apartment together, and the soft glow of Christmas lights and rose gold decorations welcome us home. "You good out here if I take a shower?" I ask as he settles onto the couch.

I don't miss the spark in his eyes—that unmistakable thirst. I know exactly what he's thinking about. All the times we've been in my shower together—the heat, the steam, the way he's touched me, claimed me, moved inside me—it's all playing out in his mind. His lips quirk slightly, like he's already considered joining me in there, ready to push this tension between us into something else entirely. A part of me aches for it, craves it, desperate to have him fuck the confusion out of my mind, but I also know I need a minute to catch my breath.

We need to talk, and anything else has to wait. We both know it, even if neither of us particularly likes it.

"I'll make us some drinks," he says, standing up and heading into the kitchen. "Then we talk, baby, yeah?" I nod and watch him disappear before making my way to the shower, relieved to finally change out of these ridiculous clothes.

My fingers fumble with the ties and clips of the festive lingerie, and I strip it off, letting it fall to the floor in a pile of green and red.

I step into the shower and the warm water cascades over me, washing away the memory of that shitty little actress with her hands on Edison. The way he had my back tonight really makes me hate that I went straight to assuming the worst. His methods might have been questionable, but he delivered his point without an ounce of shame, making damn sure Maddy knew exactly where his heart belonged.

He said he's falling in love with me, and the truth is, I'm right there with him.

After getting out of the shower, I slip into my silk robe and make my way back to Edison. He's settled comfortably on my couch, his ankle propped up on his knee, holding a glass in one hand and his phone in the other. As I get closer, he doesn't move, except for the slow lift of those silver eyes.

His gaze rakes over my body, lingering on the way the silk clings to my curves. He's already undressing me with his eyes, attempting to strip away the last layers of distance between us, and the heat of it burns through me.

"You really don't play fair, baby," he says, setting his drink down on the side table and placing his phone beside him on the couch.

"You saw me wearing a lot less twenty minutes ago."

"I wanted you then too."

"I thought you wanted to talk."

"I do, but I'm also tempted to say fuck it and have you ride my face first." I climb into his lap as he lowers his leg to make room for me.

"I need to ask you something first."

"What is it, beautiful?"

"You said something tonight."

"I said a lot of things tonight."

"You told Maddy you were falling in love with me."

His hands rest on my bare thighs, his thumbs brushing slow circles against my skin.

"I did."

"Did you say it for a reaction?"

"A reaction from her?" he asks, and I nod. He slides his hands over my ass, pulling me closer. "Absolutely fucking not." His eyes search my face as if he's trying to see straight into my mind to read every thought I'm not voicing out loud. "But I shouldn't have said it, and for that I apologize."

"Okay," I answer, though my voice betrays the uncertainty I'm trying to hide.

"Not because I don't feel it, but because you should've been the first to hear it—not with her there, but when it was just the two of us. I didn't think it through at the time."

"So, you meant it? You're... I mean, you feel that way?"

"It's not a dirty word, Sydney, but I've never told anyone I was in love with them before," he says, his voice steady. "Don't get me wrong, I've loved, without a doubt. But have I ever been *in love*?" He exhales gently, shaking his head. "No, not until you." I slide my hands around his neck, my fingers playing with the strands of hair resting there. "Listen, I know it's fast, but I think you already knew I was in love with you. You own me completely, in a way I can't shake, a way I don't ever want to escape." His hand moves slowly through my hair, pushing it back from my face, and my breath hitches as the gravity of his words sinks in. "You make me feel things I'd only ever hoped for, and I swear to you, you're it for me. There's no one else—there never will be."

Deep down, I knew. How could I not? I feel it in every touch and every kiss. I feel it in the way his fingers roam over my skin with an unspoken need—like no matter how close we get, it's never close enough.

This isn't just passion—it's full-blown possession.

"It's okay if you don't feel the same right now, but I promise you, baby, you will—because I'm never letting you go."

His confidence is unwavering, but I catch a flicker of fear in his eyes—a small shadow of doubt that maybe, just maybe, I don't feel as strongly for him as he does for me.

"Edison, I feel it," I whisper. "I wasn't looking for this, not at all. I didn't even want it. But I don't think I could've stopped myself from falling in love with you even if I tried." I swallow as my heart pounds against my chest. "And now that I have, I don't want to let it go. I want to hold onto it for as long as possible."

"How about forever because I'm all in?"

"You are?" I ask, unable to help the smile that spreads across my face.

"Yeah, Sydney. I am."

We're both high on love, like sunsets laced with heroin—intoxicating, overwhelming, almost too vivid to be real. It's the kind of love that gets under your skin, leaving you craving more—a hit that's as beautiful as it is dangerous. Every time he looks at me, it's like a shot to the veins, but I'm too far gone to care if this addiction consumes me.

"So you're my..." I trail off, and a low laugh rumbles from his chest.

"Sydney, you're mine, and I'm yours. Boyfriend, partner—whatever you want to call me, I'm yours." He takes a deep breath, and I feel my emotions rising. "I have a question I'd like to ask you now."

"Okay."

"Spend Christmas with me."

"Sounds like more of a demand."

"Maybe it is, but I'd still like your answer to be yes." His hands glide up my back, pulling me closer until we're chest to chest. "I want to wake up with you on Christmas morning in matching pajamas, right between your legs, so I can wish you a Merry Christmas with my tongue."

I can't help but give him the biggest smile as I run my hands through his dark hair, feeling the silky strands between my fingertips.

"I want it all, Sydney."

"How could I ever say no to that?"

"So you will?" he asks, his lips curling into the most irresistible smile. I nod, unable to look away as his laughter spills into the room, rich and filled with a joy so pure it feels like sunshine.

Pretty sure this man has buried himself so deeply inside me that I'll never be able to wash off the scent of his soul.

"Now that we've covered that," he says, raising his hips slightly, his erection pressing against me, letting me feel just how much he wants me.

The lust in his eyes has me climbing out of his lap. I stand up and slip off my robe, letting it fall to the floor, leaving me completely naked before him. His jaw clenches as he drinks me in, and I can practically feel his eyes devouring every inch of my skin.

He leans back on the couch, his gaze locked on me as if he's daring me to come closer. He spreads his arms across the back of the couch, a smirk tugging at his lips. His posture seems relaxed, yet there's a tension simmering beneath the surface—a tightly coiled energy that screams command and control.

"Come here," he demands, patting his lap, but I give him a defiant shake of my head. "No?" he asks, arching one perfect eyebrow as his expression becomes a mix of surprise and intrigue.

"No," I say, taking a small step back from him.

"Baby, if you don't bring that ass back over here, I'll fucking mark it."

"You won't be touching me until you beg for me, Edison."

"That right?" he murmurs as his eyes shamelessly roam over my body. I take a seat on the couch across from him, watching as his chest rises and falls, his breath coming in heavier.

I let my hands wander over my skin, teasing myself as I start with my breasts, cupping them while my fingers rub my nipples until they harden under my touch. A soft moan slips from my lips as pleasure shoots straight to my clit, my back arches slightly, and my thighs clench together. Edison's eyes darken, his jaw tightens, the room suddenly feels hotter, and I know he's imagining his hands in place of mine.

"Are you hard for me, baby?" I watch him palm the front of his pants, his hand slowly moving over the obvious bulge.

"What do you think?" he snaps, his voice filled with raw lust and frustration.

His eyes follow my hands as I lower one to my clit. I drag my middle finger over it, and his reaction is instant. He leans forward, elbows resting on his knees, hands pressed to his lips while he holds himself back.

"Spread yourself open for me. Show me how wet you are," he demands, and I bite my lip as I slide my fingers down, parting my pussy for him.

"You want a taste? Or am I making myself come tonight?" I push, knowing exactly the kind of response I'm about to get.

"Your orgasms belong to me, and you know it, so stop fucking with me."

"Unless I see you on your knees, this orgasm is mine," I taunt as I slowly circle my clit. I throw my head back, a moan spilling from my lips, getting off purely on the fact that he's watching every second of it.

"Sydney," he warns, yet I continue pushing his limits.

"Do you understand how it felt for me tonight?" His eyes lift from my hand between my thighs and fix on my face. "How out of control I felt, watching you comfort her while I felt like I was losing you." I see a flicker of regret cross his face, and I know he gets it; I know it's sinking in. "I understand what you were doing and why, but I can't help but want to punish you for the way you made me feel for those few minutes."

He's staring at me with the devil in his eyes, and I'm aching for him to let that side come out and play. But not until he's given me what I want, on my terms, with the control firmly in my hands.

"Knees, Edison. I won't ask again."

I watch him rise to his full height, every inch of him exuding a quiet dominance. His hands move to unfasten his belt, and the metallic clank cuts through the silence, holding my full attention before he sets it down.

My mouth waters as he unbuttons his shirt, revealing the beautiful tattoos that decorate his sculpted chest and the faint trail of hair leading down into his pants.

I keep touching myself while he slowly sheds the rest of his clothes, and when his cock finally springs free from his boxer briefs, I almost lose it.

He lifts his belt, but my attention is drawn to his other hand as it lowers to his cock, fingers curling around his length. I watch the relief wash over his face as he touches himself, his lips parting slightly while our eyes burn into each other.

Every stroke of his cock, every small throaty moan, feels like a challenge—like he's reminding me just how much control he has, and I realize how desperate I am to see him lose it.

He approaches me, towering over me as he grips the back of the couch and leans in close. His breath warms my skin as he drags his nose along my jaw. "I can smell how turned on you are, beautiful," he says as his other hand moves to grip my throat, his dominance making me even more needy than I already was. He knows exactly what he's doing to me; he knows how to make my body ache for release. "But if you make yourself come, you won't get my cock."

"And if I don't see you on your knees soon, then you won't get this cunt that you love so fucking much. So I might as well get myself off, don't you think?"

I tease myself slowly before picking up the pace, rubbing faster as I grind against my hand. His composure cracks bit by bit as the sight of me pleasuring myself wrecks him. His eyes darken, his jaw tenses hard, and all he can manage is a hoarse, strained "fuck."

"Stop," he demands, his voice sharp.

Part of me wants to defy him and push him further, but there's something in the way that he commands me that makes me crave submission.

My fingers are still against my clit as he lowers to his knees before me.

I lift my foot and rest it on his shoulder, feeling his powerful muscles flex beneath my toes. His hand wraps around my leg, holding me in place as he leans in close, his face pressing against my calf. He inhales deeply, almost desperately, his lips brushing against the inside of my knee before his tongue traces a heated path up my thigh.

"That's a good fucking boy," I murmur, taunting him as each word rolls off my tongue. My fingers trace along his jaw, gripping firmly as I tilt his face, forcing him to meet my eyes. "Fuck, look at you, baby. Submission suits you."

He reaches forward, grasping my wrists with his large, inked hands. "You're my fucking addiction. Do you know that?" he growls, his voice thick with need. "Do you have any idea what you do to me, Sydney?" As the heat of his words burns through me, I nod breathlessly. "Right now, I'm giving in to you and your hold over me. I'm giving into this addiction. So feed it—give me the high I'm so fucking desperate for." My body goes slack, and I feel the shift—the moment my control slips away and becomes his.

Using his belt, he wraps it tightly around my wrists and pulls it firm with his teeth. He binds me before lifting my arms above my head and securing me in place.

"I will always get on my knees for you, Sydney, because you're my goddamn queen," he rasps, his lips sucking on my inner thigh, marking me. "But depriving me of this?" he continues, sliding a finger inside me. "That doesn't happen again." I bite my lip, loving the way his eyes flare with possessiveness as his finger slowly rubs along the spot inside me that makes my body erupt. "Now, you're going to take my cock, and I'm going to fuck every last drop of my cum into this pretty little pussy. Understand?" I can only nod, my body already arching into him as it responds to his words.

I moan in frustration as he pulls his finger away, leaving me aching for him to touch me again. He raises my bound arms higher with the black belt, forcing my back to arch farther. I feel the stretch in my muscles as he tilts my hips just right and slaps his cock down on my clit. "One day, I'll put a baby in you, Sydney. But until then, I'm going to watch my cum spill out of this cunt every time I'm done fucking it."

"Edison, please," I beg, my voice laced with need. He lets his lips ghost over mine, barely touching, before pulling back with a satisfied smirk.

"Much better," he mutters. "I love how desperate you are to get fucked."

Without warning, he drives in deep, his cock stretching and filling me—the sudden intrusion a perfect blend of overwhelming pleasure tempered with just the right amount of pain. He stays buried, giving me a moment to adjust, letting me feel every pulse, every throb.

"Oh my god," I breathe out, my eyes rolling back as he fills me to the hilt.

"Fucking watch," he demands, tugging on the belt.

The pull jerks my body forward, forcing me to look down and watch where we're connected as his thrusts grow harder, driving deeper with each snap of his hips. His eyes darken as he watches us— how perfectly we fit together, how we move as one as we lose ourselves in each other.

"Look at us, baby. Nothing has ever felt like this."

"Oh god, right there." I gasp, my breath hitching as I rock my body up against his. Heat coils through me, spreading like wildfire as I match him thrust for thrust, my hips grinding up with every hit of my pussy.

My body tightens, thighs trembling and toes curling as my orgasm crashes over me. "Scream for me, Sydney," he says, cutting through my pleasure haze as I begin to unravel beneath him. "Let the neighbors hear the way your pussy begs for me to fill it."

I can't hold back—the scream rips from my throat, and his name falls from my lips as he continues to fuck me into oblivion.

"That's my girl," he murmurs as he pulls his cock out of me and dives down between my legs.

His tongue glides up my opening, swirling and tasting, collecting every last drop of my orgasm before he moves back up my body and crashes his lips against mine. His tongue thrusts into my mouth, kissing me so fucking deep and dirty, letting me taste myself on him as he devours me like a man starved.

"I wanna feel you everywhere, Edison."

His eyes search mine as he pulls back slightly, but the way his gaze darkens sends heat rippling through me. His head tilts ever so slightly, and I don't miss the faint flicker of a smirk playing on his lips. His thumb brushes against my cheek, tracing a slow path down to my jaw as if he's memorizing me and the way I look when I ask him for the one thing I know he'd love to take from me.

"You want me inside your ass, baby?" His voice is smooth, like velvet, wrapping around me as I nod, and he captures my mouth in a crushing kiss. I feel like I'm drowning in him—his taste, his scent, and the way his mouth dominates mine. "I'm going to untie you. You'll need something to hold onto." He slips the belt from around my wrists, letting it fall to the floor, and takes a moment to brush his lips softly against each wrist, his kiss soothing the slight marks. "Turn around for me, beautiful."

I follow his command as I turn on the couch. He leans in close, his tongue gliding over the damp skin of my back, tasting me and leaving a fire in its wake.

His fingers slip between my legs, finding me already wet and wanting, and he drags my slickness back, teasing the forbidden place he's ready to claim. When he presses a finger against my tight entrance, my body tenses, bracing itself as I prepare to be broken apart.

"Talk to me, Sydney."

"It feels different," I say, my voice breaking as he slowly twists his finger deep inside me. His pace quickens while his other hand finds my clit, and the two sensations make my hips buck against him. My nails dig into the back of the couch, anchoring me as he unravels me piece by piece until all that's left is his name on my lips.

Edison stands up behind me, and a needy whimper escapes my throat at the loss of his hands on my body. "I've been so fucking desperate to take this ass, Sydney. I can't wait to see what it looks like when my cum starts spilling out of you."

His words send a surge straight to my core, a pulsing need that only grows when I turn to look at him. His fingers work their way inside my pussy, each movement drawing a moan from my lips as I watch him coat himself with my arousal. Just as I feel the pressure of his tip against my entrance, my body goes haywire, as if it's losing its shit and loving every second of it.

"Jesus, Edison, you're about to tear me in half."

"I promise I'll start slow, but you can take me, baby. Just relax for me," he murmurs, but I know he's not even halfway there yet.

I suck in a sharp breath as I fight to adjust to the stretch. "I can't..."

"You fucking *are* Sydney, and it's beautiful," he urges as a guttural groan leaves his lips. The burn starts to fade, giving way to pleasure as he works himself deeper, inch by thick inch, until he's fully seated inside me.

Edison's hand wraps tightly around my hair, pulling me back against his solid chest, my spine arching as he presses me flush against him. His other hand slides to my throat, fingers curling possessively around my neck, and my pulse kicks up under his palm.

His pace quickens, each thrust deeper, harder, as his desperation grows, and he begins to unravel. His hand slips down between my thighs, finding my clit and tugging, rubbing fast circles until my eyes roll back, the tension building low in my belly.

"God, you feel so good, baby. The way your ass is taking me... knowing I'm the only man who's ever been here... fuck." He's close, the savage fucking giving away how desperate he is to own every part of me.

I feel it building, my climax winding tighter and tighter, coiling in my core like a spring on the verge of snapping. And then it hits, crashing over me and tearing a raw, animalistic sound from my throat. My body clamps down around him, spasming with every pulse of pleasure.

"Edison!"

"I'm fucking coming!"

His hips move erratically as he chases his own release, his brutal fucking of my ass all now for him, and I love it. I love that he's using my body for his every need as mini aftershocks ripple through me.

"I need your mouth," he growls, gripping my face and turning it toward him, claiming my lips in a fierce kiss. He swallows my gasps, and with one final thrust, he buries himself as deep as possible, his cock pulsing as he fills me.

He remains inside me, his cock still twitching as he keeps me stretched around him as if he's branding me from the inside out. I feel every heavy pulse of him, every slow throb that makes my body clench, keeping his cock warm and his cum right where it belongs. His breath is hot against my neck, and I can feel his heartbeat pounding in his chest, a reminder that he's still here, owning a part of me nobody ever has. When he finally starts to pull out, I feel him dragging along every nerve, and I hate the emptiness I feel as he slips free. Before I can process, I feel two of his fingers pressing back into my ass, pushing his cum that started to leak back inside me.

"Marked and fucking claimed," he says, and I swear I can feel every word vibrate against my skin. "Every beautiful inch of you is mine, and I love you."

Epilogue

Edison

Every Christmas Eve, my wife sleeps beside me, completely naked—though, to be honest, she's rarely in clothes when we're in this bed. It's a complete waste of everyone's time when all I'm going to do is strip her out of them anyway. Every year, without fail, I wake her up right on the edge of her orgasm. Sometimes, I'm inside her, fucking her slow and deep until her moans pull her out of sleep. Other times, my mouth is on her—like now—my tongue circling her clit and dipping inside her, tasting just how wet she gets for me even when she's dreaming.

This is our third Christmas together, our second since becoming a married couple, and each year, my hunger for her only grows. The way she still loses herself in me gives me a craving that only deepens. It's an obsession that I swear only gets stronger every day.

And yeah, I very quickly became a "flowers and diamonds" kinda guy.

Only this year, as I run my hands across my wife's body, my fingers trace the swell of her stomach, where our daughter has been growing for the past six months. It's softer, fuller, and more beautiful than ever.

Getting pregnant hasn't been straightforward for us. We've gone through months of waiting and hoping, and yeah, I had the best time trying to put a baby in her, but there were moments when Sydney found it tough. However, my strong girl never gave up. She never stopped believing that one day we'd be blessed.

She's not only my wife but the mother of my child, and god, if that doesn't make me feel everything all at once. There's this pride that swells inside me every time I look at her and see the change happening to her body.

It's like she's unlocked this whole new level of beauty—she's breathtaking.

Three months after the night I first told Sydney I was in love with her, she was living with me. She never went back to the club, and by the following Christmas, I'd made her my wife.

I've never been as sure about anything as I am about Sydney.

My soulmate.

My obsession.

My forever.

I should've known she was the one before she clawed her way inside me and reminded me that I'm still breathing,

Before she gripped my soul and rode it bare.

I fought like hell for her, and I fucking won.

As she starts to stir, I pin her thighs to the bed, gripping her tighter, making sure she wakes up knowing she's not going anywhere until I suck every ounce of pleasure from her. She's mine to satisfy, and I'm not stopping until she's shaking. Sometimes, my wife gets greedy and continues to grind against my face after she comes, and fuck, if I don't love seeing her so damn needy for me.

I'd happily spend all of Christmas in this bed, but we always go to her mom's, and as much as I would love to keep Sydney here, I'm not willing to piss off my mother-in-law if I can help it.

She's just as terrifying as Sydney can be, and I've got a feeling our daughter is going to be the exact same way.

"Edison," she gasps as her fingers find my hands, which are resting beside her stomach. Her fingers link with mine, and her back arches as I suck her clit into my mouth, loving how sensitive she is with all these fresh hormones coursing through her.

"Merry Christmas, baby," I say with a smile, just before my tongue dips inside her.

"Oh God, I'm close." She writhes, and her body thrashes beneath me. I keep my grip firm on her, my tongue relentless as I push her closer to the edge. Within seconds, she cries out my name and gifts me the screams I've been waiting for as she shakes under my hold.

"Fucking beautiful." I press a kiss to her clit, causing her to flinch and let out a laugh. I start kissing my way up her body, and when I reach her mouth, I grasp her chin and tilt her head back. "Open," I command, and I thrust my tongue inside her mouth, kissing her deeply and pouring all my love for her into it.

"Are you ready for our last Christmas with just the two of us?" she asks, her fingers threading through my hair. I lay beside her, my head resting against her chest and my hand lowering to her stomach.

"Maybe we should stay here today," I suggest as my hand slides lower and strokes the curve of her hip. "Because if it's our last, then I'd really like to have you all to myself."

"We can't just leave Nick and Cora at my mom's. Besides, do you really want to deal with Grace's wrath?"

"Fuck no, but I want to spend the day buried inside you, taking my time, fucking you slowly, making you feel every inch until you need me to make you come more than you need your next breath."

I run my nose along her jawline and inhale her scent. "Then I'll fuck you roughly, and watch you come undone as I tear you apart." Her body erupts into goosebumps, and I smirk, knowing exactly what my words are doing to her. "Tell me you don't want that, baby? Because I'm so fucking hard for you."

She grabs my hand and presses it between her legs. "Of course I fucking want that." I slide a finger inside her, feeling how wet she still is. "I'd say you've got about an hour before we need to start getting ready and head to my mom's. So if you want inside me, Edison, then I suggest you take me already." She rocks her hips against my hand as her body practically begs me for more, and that's all the invitation I need.

THE END

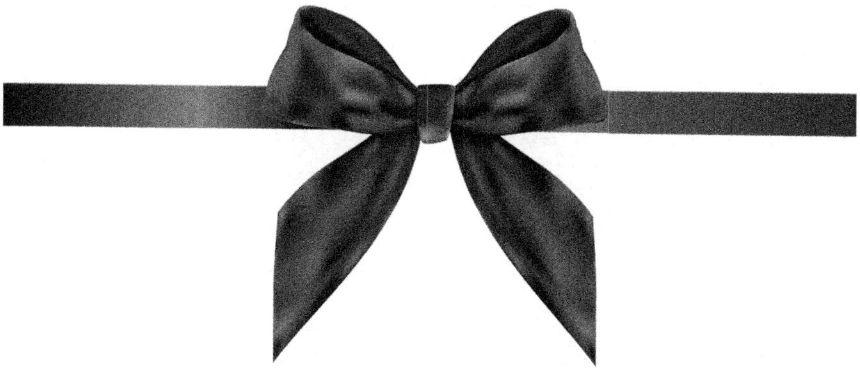

Acknowledgements

Firstly, thank you for reading *His for Christmas*. I really hope you enjoyed this spicy little novella.

As always, my biggest thanks go to my husband and babies. I'll be forever thankful for your support of this little dream of mine.

A special thank you to my family. This time around, you've been part of the journey with me. Your support has impacted me more than I could ever put into words.

To my amazing friends who keep me grounded and are always there when I need them—thank you for being some of my absolute favorite people in the world.

To the incredible girls on my street team—where would I be without you? I can't thank you all enough for your support, encouragement, and the way you share my books and help me get my little stories out into the world. You lift me up when I'm struggling, and for that, I'm so grateful. Oh, and you're all stuck with me forever!

To my fantastic editing team, just like last time, you've been incredible. I can't wait to work with you again in a few months!

And finally, thank you to the community of authors and readers. You've all played a huge role in helping me live my dream, and I appreciate you more than you know.

Love, Lea xx

About the Author

Lea Rose is a contemporary romance author who writes about strong, women and men who'd drop to their knees for them. She loves a good slow burn with a twist of angst, and you can always expect a happy ever after. When she's not immersed in the universes her characters reside in, Lea loves nothing more than to sit down with a book and read to her heart's content. Of course, that's only if she's not busy chasing after her kids or binge-watching a TV series with her husband.

Connect with Lea on Instagram: @authorlearose
Website: Learose.net

ALSO BY LEA ROSE

Breaking The Rules Series

Until We Meet Again – Book One

After All This Time – Book Two (Coming February 14th 2025)
Pre-order Available on Amazon

Printed in Great Britain
by Amazon